An empty bottle of Haig and Haig rested on the floor on the rider's side in the front, unbroken, the sole ironic survivor of the trip. The driver was not so lucky; a young blond woman crushed against and into the steel and glass of the smashed auto, a limp rag doll barely containing her stuffing, with the doll-face turned toward us, pretty much intact, eyes mercifully closed.

"Christ," I said. I leaned against the wreckage and looked away. Looked out toward where the river was supposed to be, but through the trees and blackness I could see nothing, though the presence of the river was there, in the soft but distinct sounds of waves lapping, lapping.

Brennan snorted, disgusted by my reaction. "Seen a hell of a lot worse," he said.

"So has he," John said. "What is it, Mal?"

"The woman. In the car."

"What? Who? Somebody you know . . . ?"

"Somebody I just met."

Look for all these Tor books by Max Allan Collins

A Mallory Novel
NO CURE FOR DEATH

Nate Heller Novels
TRUE CRIME
TRUE DETECTIVE

MAX ALLAN COLLINS
NO CURE FOR DEATH

A Mallory Novel

TOR

A TOM DOHERTY ASSOCIATES BOOK

This is a work of fiction. All the characters and events portrayed in this book are fictional, and any resemblance to real people or incidents is purely coincidental.

NO CURE FOR DEATH

Copyright © 1983 by Max Allan Collins

All rights reserved, including the right to reproduce this book or portions thereof in any form.

Reprinted by arrangement with Walker Publishing Company, Inc.

First Tor printing: April 1987

A TOR Book

Published by Tom Doherty Associates, Inc.
49 West 24 Street
New York, N.Y. 10010

ISBN: 0-812-50157-8
CAN. ED.: 0-812-50158-6

Library of Congress Catalog Card Number: 85-51186

Printed in the United States of America

0 9 8 7 6 5 4 3 2 1

*This book is for
Richard Yates,
who gave me my start back at
the Writers Workshop at Iowa City.*

AUTHOR'S NOTE

This is in no way an attempt to do a historical novel about the '70s—they are too close to us for that.

Still, the early '70s haunt us, and that era—the Vietnam era—was just winding down, as this story begins.

PART ONE

NOVEMBER 26, 1974

TUESDAY

ONE

He had the kind of face that said, "Hate me," and I wasn't arguing.

Let's just say he made a bad first impression, and I don't really think his being black had anything to do with it, though the missing eye and jagged stitched scar running above and below the empty socket sure did. His head was totally hairless—not just bald, but no eyebrows, either—and his mouth was frozen open, a down-slanting hole showing only the lower row of crooked yellow teeth, and the overall effect of his formidable visage was that of an eightball come to life—and a very mean, very ugly eightball at that—on the lookout for a white cueball to knock around.

The body below the face was equally menacing and seemed to have trouble just squeezing through the doorway of Port

City's cubicle-size bus terminal. He was huge, an exaggeration, more a cartoon than a man, like that guy in the leopard skin who tags along with Mandrake the Magician, or Daddy Warbucks's jinni strong-arm Punjab. He turned one bloodshot eye loose on the room, and I worked at making myself inconspicuous, though I felt like I was in a closet trying to convince a murder-intent cuckold I was a coat hanger.

The guy was a stranger to me, but I had the paranoid feeling that he'd been sent by somebody somewhere to make up for some nameless forgotten foul deed I'd once done, maybe in another life. Not that I was alone in the tiny waiting room, although Meyer, the depot man, was out for coffee. There was a young woman next to me on the bench, a young blonde with a tired but attractive face. But she looked innocent enough, hardly the type who'd have somebody like this out to get her.

I'd been trying, incidentally, for the previous half hour to strike up a conversation with her, as she was slender and well-formed and appealed to me as much as Punjab didn't. Besides, I've always been partial to blondes, even with roots. But I hadn't got nerve up to make my move; too shy, I guess—and too shy, too, to go rushing over to Punjab when he rolled in to express my instinctual dislike for him.

It didn't take long, not as long as it

seemed anyway, for that one eye to pick out which of us it was looking for. He drove his truck body over to where the blonde and I were sitting and planted himself in front of her, a big paw nervously smoothing the coat of his surprisingly well-tailored, well-pressed suit—custom-cut from a houndstooth tent, no doubt. A noise came rumbling up out of the depths of his throat and became something that sounded vaguely like "Bitch."

My ears discounted that, and I looked away. He seemed to know her, after all, and who was I to get involved in an argument between friends?

But it must have been "Bitch" after all, because the noise came out again, and this time was distinctly "Bitch," and louder, and part of a sentence: "Get on your damn feet, bitch, we got business."

There was terror in her face, which didn't surprise me, but there was also an unmistakable lack of recognition, which did. She'd obviously never seen her one-eyed "business" partner before—he'd been just as much a black bolt-from-the-blue for her as for me.

And he was impatient.

He grabbed up a bunch of fuzzy blue sweater in a bulky fist and lifted her off the bench and I hit him in the throat.

He did three things.

He released the girl.

He touched, lightly, his Adam's apple.

He knocked me across the room into an upright Pepsi machine, with a fly-swat backhand.

My hands groped behind me, feeling the cold metal of the soft drink machine, searching for something to grip to push to my feet. I got off my knees and started up and watched his huge body come slowly toward me in a sway reminiscent of the Frankenstein monster, and I ducked and his hamhock fist put a dent in the Pepsi machine big enough to hold a political rally in.

But that was only one of his hands, and it left him another to give me a second fly-swat, and then I was on the floor again, waiting for whatever was coming, my hands scrambling aimlessly across the surface of anything.

Where the empty Pepsi bottle came from I couldn't say, but it was in one of my hands now, and that was good enough for me. I got my eyes working and saw him barreling toward me with that reflecting skull lowered and charging and I laid the bottle across it.

He went down.

And out.

I covered my mouth with my hand and then took the hand away and looked at it. Some blood, but not too bad. I jiggled some teeth with a finger and found them safe, if not sound. My feet were under me, shaky but under me, and I leaned against the machine. Punjab lay on his stomach like a tree I had chopped down.

The young woman was sitting back on the bench, almost as though nothing had happened, although she'd turned very, very white. She was looking directly at me. "Are you all right?" she said.

I nodded and went over to the pay phone hanging on the wall by the Pepsi machine and dropped a dime in.

"Sheriff Brennan, please," I said.

"Who's calling . . ."

"Tell him Mallory."

A few moments later Brennan was on the line, saying, "Mallory, it's nearly seven o'clock. You and John should've been here fifteen, twenty minutes ago. What's the holdup?"

"John's bus is late."

"Well, come on over to the jailhouse when he gets in. Been too damn long since I seen the boy."

"John's bus being a few minutes late isn't exactly why I called." Down on the floor nearby, Punjab was stirring, just starting to shake himself out of it. "Just a second, Brennan."

"What . . . ?"

I let the phone hang loose and reached down for the bottle I'd used on Punjab, broke it against the edge of the Pepsi machine and stood there with the jagged half that was left in my hand, like a tough guy in an old B-movie. The rousing bear pushing up from the floor with his hands took it all in with that single penetrating eye of his.

That eye followed me back over to the phone, which I spoke into, the makeshift weapon in my free hand.

"Sheriff," I said, with some dramatic emphasis on the word, "suppose I told you a guy bigger than a bus rolled into the terminal and tried to run me over?"

Brennan's voice said, "What the hell . . . ?"

And Punjab was up and gone. Like maybe he'd borrowed one of his namesake's flying carpets.

Brennan's voice was saying, "What the hell's going on there?"

"Easy, Sheriff, just kidding around. Stay put and I'll bring your stepson around soon as his bus pulls in."

"Listen you spaced-out creep, if this is your idea of a joke . . ."

I put the receiver back and walked over to a wooden empty bottles case and stuck my half-a-one gently in a hole.

Meyer, who's a runty guy of twenty-six or so whom I play poker with occasionally, shuffled quickly in from his hourly coffee break at the café next door. His eyes were portholes. "Did you see the size of that guy?" he wanted to know.

I touched my still bleeding mouth with the tip of my sweat shirt. "What guy?" I said.

Meyer gave me the same sort of look he gives me when he wonders if I'm bluffing (I usually am, but don't tell Meyer) and got behind his desk and started reading the new *Penthouse*.

I glanced over at the bench and took a look at the stakes of the fight in which I'd played feeble knight to Punjab's heavyweight dragon.

She was still looking white, very, and she was shivering, rubbing her arms as if the steaming hot pipes next to her were an air conditioner, and as though her arms were bare and not in the long sleeves of her sweater.

I walked over to her.

TWO

And sat back down next to her on the bench.

I said, "Mallory."

Her eyes went from half-lidded to round, and I saw that they were blue and rather glazed. She said: "Pardon?"

"My name. That's what it is."

"Oh. Right." Air emptied out of her, a delayed reaction from the tension of the confrontation moments before. The glaze lifted off her eyes and they seemed relieved, though still tired, and somehow old. Her hands came out and reached my hands and clutched them tightly in a cold grasp. She managed a smile, not much of one, but a smile.

I said, "What's yours?"

She released my hands, taken mildly aback. "My what?"

11

"Name."

"Oh." She swallowed. "Janet. Janet Taber."

"Hello, Janet."

"Sorry I'm so dopey. I'm just a little shook, I guess."

"Understandable. Feel the same myself."

"What . . . what did you say your name was?"

"Mallory. Mal."

"Mal. Hello, Mal."

"Hello. How would you like a cup of hot coffee, Janet?"

"Oh . . ."

"I noticed you shivering. Come on. We can duck in Johnny's next door and grab a couple cups."

"I do have a bus to catch."

"Meyer over there'll come get us." I looked over at Meyer, who was slumped behind his desk studying the *Penthouse*. "Won't you, Meyer?"

He said, "Screw you, Mallory."

"That's his way of saying yes," I said. "Now, what do *you* say?"

She smiled. Full out. It was a nice smile; she didn't look quite so tired, so prematurely old, when she smiled that way.

She brushed some blond hair out of her face and said, "Okay."

Two minutes later we were together in Johnny's Grille in a back booth, both sitting on one side, snuggled together, almost like lovers. But there wasn't much sex in it, really; just the closeness of two people who have shared something, which we certainly had, thanks to Punjab.

"How can I thank you?" she said.

"You can't," I said. "A hero like me comes along once per damsel-in-distress lifetime."

Martha, the manager of the place, who also waited tables during slow times, stopped by the booth and I asked for a couple coffees.

Janet touched my hand. "Would you mind terribly if I had hot chocolate instead?"

I grinned, shrugged and made the correction, opting for hot chocolate myself. When I looked at her I saw she was grinning too. A playful grin, and even with the wan face with its prematurely deep lines 'round eyes and mouth, and roots marring the beauty of blond hair that swept around her face in two gentle arcs, the eyes that had an old woman in them, even with all of that, she was a child. A child who'd walked home from school in a snowstorm and when the winter dark began to fall, got scared and cold; when she finally got home her mother fixed her hot chocolate and then she was better. That kind of child.

"I-never-saw-that-horrible-man-before-in-my-life," she said suddenly, "ever."

"Listen," I said, "don't feel obligated to tell me anything you don't want to. No explanations necessary." In a way I meant it: momentary heroism or not, pretty blonde or no, I had no driving compulsion to "get involved." As if I wasn't already.

"I'm telling you the truth, Mal."

"I believe you, Janet."

"It's just that it must seem kind of unbelievable to you that something like that could just walk in out of nowhere and accost somebody."

"Not so unbelievable. I just experienced it myself, remember? It must've been some weird mistaken identity trip, that's all."

"It must have." She looked at me, reached for my hand and squeezed: she sensed my disbelief, evidently, despite my claims to the contrary. "I'm not putting you on, Mal. I never saw him before, and I don't know anyone who'd have any reason for sending somebody like that."

"I said I believe you, Janet." And I was almost starting to.

"Christ, he was big. And that eye . . . the one that . . . wasn't there. Brrrrrr. I have to say you handled yourself well, Mal. It must not be the first fight you were ever in."

"No."

"You know, sometimes when I'm waiting by myself, at a bus stop or in a reception room, I sometimes play a game of trying to guess people from their looks—I guess that's something everybody does, huh? But that's what I was doing with you while we were sitting in the terminal. . . ."

Martha came with our hot chocolate and I said thanks and Janet continued. "Anyway," she said sipping, "I couldn't get a reading on you. Nothing. Not a thing."

I blew some heat off the chocolate. "You could've guessed anything and probably hit something I've been one time or another."

"Just what are you now?"

"Have to tell you?"

"Have to."

"A college student. Of sorts."

"You're kidding."

"Not at all. Right now I'm on quarter break. Thanksgiving vacation."

"Come on."

"I know, I know. I look a little weathered for a college boy. Well, I'm not twenty-five yet, I'll have you know, and people a hell of a lot older than that go to college."

"Don't be so defensive about it. I didn't mean you seemed too old or anything . . . you just don't look the college type. How'd you end up that way?"

"Ran out of other things, I guess. I was in Vietnam a short tour, got wounded and sent home. I worked construction. I was a cop for a while, a little while, tried newspaper work, tended bar, finally dropped out, as they used to say, and was into the dope thing, briefly. Things were seeming kind of pointless, so I tried coming home and starting over. Been back since August, started school in September."

"And you're not putting me on? You were a cop, and a doper, too?"

"I just saved your rear end, lady, would I put you on? Besides, wait till you hear what I do for a living."

"Oh? What's that?"

"I write mystery stories."

"You're kidding!"

"No, really. Although saying I make a living out of it may be stretching a point."

"You mean, like you write books?"

"Not yet. But I've been selling short stories to *Ellery Queen* and *Mike Shayne*. Those are mystery magazines."

"I'm impressed," she said, meaning it, smiling.

"Don't be," I said. "What about you? Janet Taber? What's the story of *your* life?"

It was like a shadow came over her face. The brightness, the child in her was gone, and she looked tired again and the old woman was back in her eyes.

"Janet? Hey, I didn't mean to bring you down. . . ."

She shook her head; the hot chocolate in her hands shook, too, spilled a little. "Christ, *self-pity* brings you down after a while. Listen, if I went into all of it, it's just a friggin' bore, real bummer, the depression that comes with it and all."

I held up a hand. "Any way you want it, Janet."

"You don't mind? I just rather not go into any of that."

"Hell, no—unless," I said, and I slurped at my hot chocolate late for dramatic effect, "unless maybe there's something back there in what you don't want to think about, and don't want to talk about, that's . . . dangerous."

She got my meaning and started to stiffen up. "I told you I never saw him before."

"And I told you I believe you."

"Well . . ." She stared down into her mug of chocolate. "I got to admit it isn't the only strange thing that's happened to me lately."

"Oh?"

"Well, not to me exactly. To my mother."

"Your mother?"

"That's what the bus is all about. I live here in Port City, have lately at least. I'm going up this afternoon to Iowa City, to the University Hospital."

"I don't follow you, Janet."

"My mother. That's where she is. The hospital."

"I'm sorry. What's the trouble?"

"She's dying, I'm afraid."

"You want to tell me about it?"

She sipped at the mug of chocolate calmly and told me that somebody had beaten her mother half to death and set the house on fire and left the old lady to burn.

THREE

"I'd been living for the last four or five years with a guy in Chicago—a guy I met during my first and last year at Drake in Des Moines. We weren't married, but it was more than a shack-up thing, you know. We, uh, had a kid, and you know, stuck it out together.

"We were part of the Old Town scene—he turned out pop art paintings and sold 'em on the street and through various shops, and I clerked in a bookstore—just a couple hippies with a love child, right? Gradually we both got into drugs, him kind of heavy, me not so—I found I couldn't let go of the idea I was supposed to be a 'good mother' to my child.

"The kid was getting along fine, until one day he—by this time he was about three-and-a-half—he started acting sickly.

Short of breath all the time, and complaining sometimes about chest pain. I took the kid to a doctor—and from the doctor to a specialist, and found that he had a heart condition that . . . that could eventually require surgery. Boy, did *I* come down quickly out of that druggie fantasy-world. I immediately started making mental lists of the changes that would have to take place in my life; that night I tried to tell my soulmate what the score was and he said, 'no more fuckin' hassles,' and walked out. I haven't seen him since.

"The moment the door closed behind my ex, I reached for the phone and called my mother and started pouring it all out. It'd been years since I talked to her, years since I'd dropped out of college, turned runaway, moved to Old Town and had a kid and all. I'd hardly got a word out when Mom told me that Dad died three years ago. I . . . I slammed the receiver down and waited for the tears, but there weren't any, so I laughed instead. The kind of laughing that doesn't have a damn thing to do with being happy, y'know? And, after the laughter, I thought of suicide. Real seriously thought of suicide. But my kid came first, before any such luxury, so I picked the phone up again and called Mom back."

She stopped, and I thought for a moment she was going to break down; her one hand clutched the cup of hot chocolate, the other was on the table, trembling. My instinct was to hold that trembling hand—to give her some support. I didn't know her well enough to do that, of course—but then we'd been through a war together, hadn't we? A one-eyed war, so I followed my instinct and took her hand, and she gave me a quivery little smile that said she hadn't taken my gesture the wrong way, and she got her story going again.

"Mom said she could help me, help *us*, my kid and me, but she also said certain arrangements would be necessary and that she would call me later, after the . . . arrangements were made. Four hours dragged by. Then the phone rang again, and I picked it up and it was Mom. What my mother told me seemed strange to me, but I didn't argue. I was glad for the help. Anyway, she said I wasn't to come to Des Moines—that's where my family always lived—but was to meet her at an address in Port City. I didn't know she'd even ever *been* to Port City. But that was where we'd be living from here on out, according to Mom. She wouldn't explain why, only said she'd tell me more later, after we were settled in."

Here she paused again, looking down into the cup of hot chocolate like she was looking for tea leaves to read.

"What I later found out was that an 'old

friend of the family' who lived in Port City was interested in my kid, and wanted to make sure the boy was given the 'best possible care.' Those words: best possible care. Only this old friend wanted to remain anonymous. I had an idea who this person was, but I thought I better not make waves . . . at least not when I found out my boy was to be sent to this famous clinic, in New York.

"Still, several things were really bothering me. Mom and me were supposed to stay in Port City. We weren't to follow the boy back east to the clinic. There was no reason given for this, it was just a . . . condition. And so as to stay as anonymous as possible, our benefactor *insisted* on making all his arrangements with Mom—that made me *sure* I knew who it was but Mom always denied it. I . . . never pressed the issue. My kid came first."

Now her voice started to catch every few words; the blue eyes were moist.

"Last night . . . last night I spent the evening with a friend of mine. Since I didn't have a car, my friend offered to drive me home, to Mom's house, where I've been living. Half . . . half a dozen blocks from home the air started to fill with black smoke. The sky was . . . it was orange. Our house was in flames."

She was squeezing my hand, now; she didn't seem to know she was, but she was.

"I . . . I jumped from the car before it even stopped, and started running. As I was running I saw a couple firemen trying to carry a burning sofa out of the . . . the blaze. On the sofa was . . . was what I could only make out as a . . . ch-charred lump. Which the firemen put from the sofa onto a stretcher, to put it in the ambulance that was backed up on the sidewalk. I looked closer, and . . . the charred lump . . . was Mom."

And now she cried. Finally she cried.

I started. "You don't have to . . ."

But she went on. Choking back the tears, their wet trails shiny on her face, like thin narrow ribbons.

"Mom's hair was burned off, only short black stalks of it were still there. Her skin was showing through the burned strips of clothing that were on her, and h-her skin was ash-gray, where it wasn't black. Her face was so . . . so burned it swelled three times normal size. It . . ."

"Stop, Janet," I said. "Don't put yourself through this." I'd taken a paper napkin and was dabbing at her face, drying the tears like a parent; she didn't seem to know I was doing it.

"They didn't let me ride in the ambulance with her. They said she had to go to the University Hospital in Iowa City, where they have this burn unit. They sent me to my friend's house to stay the night; a doctor came with me to give me sedation, but I wouldn't let him. Five hours later I called the hospital and a doctor told me that my mother's condition was critical, but that there was something weird about the nature of her condition. There were definite signs that led them to believe my mother was beaten—*badly*—before the fire."

And she looked at me with blue eyes that weren't moist anymore; they were cold and clear and, somehow, frightened and frightening at the same time.

Then Meyer came in, and said her bus was there. She got up quickly to go, and I followed along, getting in a couple quick questions, getting back a couple quick answers. One of them was "Yes" when I asked if she'd call me when she got back from Iowa City, and let me know how she and her mother were making out.

Then she was just this pale sad face in a bus window, gliding away from me.

FOUR

Ten minutes after Janet Taber's bus left for Iowa City, John's bus pulled in.

He stepped off the bus, two heavy bags in each hand and a clothes bag over one arm, and the smile under his sunglasses said he saw me. The sunglasses were wrap-around goggles, two huge silver mirrors reflecting the sun, and the smile was John's usual white dazzler, so the main impression of him at first glance was all sunglasses and teeth.

Not that the rest of him wasn't striking at first glance: there was the way he was dressed, too. He had on black leather pants and a yellow-dyed buckskin coat—they were big on the West Coast for a week or two that year—with the longest hanging fringe I'd seen since the day Roy Rogers came to town when I was six. An open-collared blue shirt was showing under the coat, and a gaudy multicolor scarf was tied in a confident knot around his neck. Only his short black hair, his erect posture and the stride he used as he approached me might tip you to his being an Army sergeant arriving home on leave.

We clasped hands firmly and used our free hands to grip each other's shoulder.

"Hello, Mal."

I looked at his clothes and shook my head and laughed, and that patented smile of his gradually fizzled into an embarrassed grin.

"John," I said, "you *do* tend to overcompensate when you're out of uniform, don't you?"

"Come on, I've been stationed in California, Mal, you know that." His smile edged over onto one side of his mouth. "And I've always been one for mixing with the natives."

"Don't give me that crap," I said. "You dress like that hoping some hard case in a bar'll call you a hippie and hand you an excuse for breaking a table over his head."

"Mal, you don't really think that."

"Of course, some of it may have to do with a uniform not having the charm it once had for those young California girls."

"Maybe a little," he admitted.

That was not to mention, I thought, the certain kind of girl a uniform still can

attract in California, something John had
learned all too readily out there several
years before, prior to our leaving for his
first (and my last) Vietnam tour. Like too
many guys to mention, John got hit by one
of those pretty hustlers who marry service
men, milk them while they're overseas and
then divorce them. In John's case it was
even worse: his had a kid by somebody
else while he was gone, which didn't do
his head a lot of good.

I reached down and picked up one of his
bags and left him with the other bag and
the clothes-carrier. He gathered them up,
then turned and looked across the four
lanes of Mississippi Drive, standing on his
toes to see beyond the railroad tracks to
the waterfront parking lot, where the edge
of the river was lapping up onto the
cement incline. The river was smooth today. John turned back and his smile said
glad-to-be-home, and he said, "You got a
car, kid?"

"Yeah, it's up the block."

"Lead the way."

"Forward march, you mean?"

"Don't get cute."

We walked a few steps and John said,
"Is it cold, or am I just used to that sunny
weather?"

"It's cold."

"Why're you stopping?"

I had stopped in front of a battered

yellow Rambler, three or four years old. "Because," I said, "this is my car."

"This is your car."

"That's right."

"You're serious."

"I'd have to be."

We stowed his stuff in the back and John said, "Whatever made you pick a self-proclaimed lemon like this?"

"Saves money on gas," I shrugged. "And it didn't cost much to begin with."

"But I thought your folks left you a bundle, Mal. And since when are you frugal?"

"Jesus, you Army types are a tactful lot, ain't ya?"

I got behind the wheel and John got in on the other side and I pulled out of the parking place and drove half a block and waited at a red light.

"Tell you the truth," I said, "I went through a lot of that cash my folks left me in the first year after they died. One of the things I wasted it on was one of those damn fiberglass 'Vettes, which I totaled within a month of buying it. Lately I've decided to make my money last a while, what's left of it, so I can coast as long as possible without succumbing to taking— how you say?—gainful employment."

The light went to green and I turned right on Second.

John said, "I had an M/G out in California for a few months. The payments broke me, and the speeding tickets didn't help, either. I was even in jail once."

"How fast were you going?"

"Hundred 'n' forty. I was dressed like this, you know? They treated me like garbage, until they found out I was an Army sergeant and then they almost apologized for stopping me. Hypocritical bastards."

"But that was after they jailed you?"

"Just overnight. Didn't have any identification on me. Jail was no big deal after living over one as long as I did."

"That reminds me, your stepdad wants to see you. Want to swing by his office?"

"Naw," he said, "just as soon grab a beer or something first. How about we go out to your place and shoot the bull?"

"Fine."

We started up the gradual hill that Second Street turns into as it leads into the part of town called East Hill. Port City's your typical quiet little middle-class, industrial river town, with twenty-some thousand residents, whose only mild claim to fame is having a famous ex-resident in Mark Twain. As Sam Clemens, Twain used to edit the *Port City Journal* and had a house along the river front that he said in later years provided the most beautiful front-porch view of the sun setting on the Mississippi he had ever seen; a couple years ago the old house was torn down to make way for a Skelly station.

I wondered if Janet Taber really would call me when she got back. It wasn't just that she was attractive, though that had something to do with it; but the story she'd told me about her mother and the house burning down, not to mention my encounter with that one-eyed nightmare in the terminal, made her rather like the beginning of a fascinating serial running in a magazine, the kind where you're afraid you might screw up somehow and miss the next issue.

"I said the town hasn't changed much," John said.

"What?"

"Christ, two years to catch up on and all you can do is sit there daydreaming."

"Oh. Sorry, John. Just thinking."

"This is where I'm supposed to say, 'What's her name?' "

I grinned.

"Nice?" he asked.

"Not bad. She's been through all hell lately, so she wasn't looking her best, I'd wager."

"Want to talk about it?"

I pulled onto Grand Avenue, which brought us within a few blocks of my trailer, and said, "Do you believe in hate at first sight?" And I told him about Punjab.

The Rambler and my account of the bus station brawl sputtered to a simultaneous halt in front of my housetrailer. John kind of grinned when he saw the trailer, but that didn't bother me.

I liked my trailer.

I didn't mind that it was a dinosaur of its kind. Just because its dull aluminum hull was battered here and there didn't mean it lacked a heart—didn't you ever see *The Wizard of Oz*?—and it was roomy for its age, probably the biggest model made during its period of our distant history. The old guy who lived in it before me obviously thought a lot of it, too, having used it as a lake cottage for years and years, then hauling it up onto this landfill vacant lot and moving in for good after his wife died. He had taken the time and expense to panel the walls, and put in a modern kitchenette. In fact, if the old boy hadn't died, he'd probably still be in it, but his son, who I bought it from, hadn't been nearly so sentimentally attached to it.

"Going to bunk in with me?" I asked John, wondering whether or not to haul his stuff inside.

"No. I better stay with Brennan. You can drive me over there later, if you don't mind."

"Sure."

We started across the big yard, all its

grass brown now with oncoming winter, toward the trailer. Even with its good size, the trailer looked small on the large and otherwise empty plot of land—an over-sized beer can littering an undersized park. The neighborhood was otherwise middle-class residential, and my trailer was out of place—but nobody had wanted to build on the experimental landfill my trailer sat on. I figured that only after thirty years or so passed without my trailer sinking into the ooze would the folks I rented my space from want to move me out so somebody could build.

John and I made our way through the door and into my living room, which was cluttered with books and records and plates of half-eaten food.

"As you can see," I said, "I spruced the joint up for you."

John didn't hear me; he was still thinking over the bus station brawl I'd just told him about.

I scooped up some of the plates and dumped them in my sink. John sat on the couch and glanced around at the posters covering my dark walls: a *2001* movie one-sheet; Jane Fonda in her pre-political Barbarella days; and a fantastic panorama called "Disneyland After Dark," depicting an orgy attended by all the Walt Disney characters. None of this fine fantasy caught

John's notice; he was still mulling over my tall tale.

I grabbed a couple Pabsts out of the icebox and tossed him one, put a record by my favorite rock group of the moment—Deep Purple—on my turntable, sat down next to him, and changed the subject.

"How long you going to be home?"

"Huh?"

"I said, how long you going to be home?"

"Oh. A month."

"Then you're going to re-up?"

"Yeah. I mean, no."

"I thought you were a career soldier, boy."

"I am. I'm going into Air America."

"The hell you say! You, a mercenary? You're kidding."

"No. I like combat. There's still action in Asia. I want some."

"You like combat *pay*, you mean. Or do you just have a death wish?"

John was stationed at a base called the "Rose Garden" (as in I-never-promised-you-a) and had been running missions along the Thailand and Vietnam border. As far as most Americans knew, our troops were out of the Vietnam conflict; but that just wasn't really the case. Still, even the "Rose Garden" would be closing its gates soon, and soldiers like John, who, crazy as it seems, *wanted* combat, would have to go the mercenary route to stay in the game.

He said, "I don't want to talk about it, Mal."

"I know, I know. Your ex-wife racked up debts you got to pay. And combat pay with Air America beats hell out of Uncle Sam's stateside duty pay. And you don't want to start civilian life in debt. I know all the reasons, but it's still crazy."

"Do me a favor."

"I won't. I'm going to bitch about this the whole month you're home. I don't have so many friends that I can afford losing one."

"Do me a favor."

"Okay. You just got here, I realize that. You want to relax, I know, I know. I'll back off. For now."

"Thanks."

"You're welcome. But going back *is* crazy, John."

John ignored me, sipped his beer. "Ever stop to wonder what's going to happen if you run into that guy again?"

"What guy?"

"That black guy at the station."

"That's a possibility better left unthought of."

"Maybe. Maybe you better talk to Brennan about it."

"Oh, Christ. That's all I need. Listen, you give me your word you won't mention this to him? I mean, he's going to want to know about that phone call I made to him

and I'm going to give him some phony
song-and-dance, so don't go messing me up
with the truth."

"I won't tell him anything, Mal."

"Good man."

"Are you sure this blonde didn't know
the guy?"

"She said not."

"Well, I don't know. Anything she said
make you think maybe somebody might
have cause to sic him on her?"

I hesitated.

What Janet had told me was kind of in
confidence, and with John's stepdad being
sheriff . . .

But John and I had always been open
with each other and I wanted to keep him
open with me, since I wanted to score
some points with him and eventually talk
him out of going in with the mercenaries
and back to Indochina. So I told him what
Janet Taber had told me.

"Jesus," John said. "Has she talked to
the police? If her mother really was beat-
en . . ."

"I assume she will," I said. "She did say
that the local people are investigating for
possible arson."

"The mother may have some answers,"
John said.

"If the old lady is in as bad a shape as
Janet said she was, I got my doubts about
her ever answering *anything* again—in this

world, anyway. How about we sit around and swap war atrocities to brighten things up a little?"

From my stereo, Deep Purple said, "Hush . . . hush . . ."

John rose and went over to the icebox and got himself a fresh Pabst. "I think she was putting you on," he said, returning to his spot on the couch. "You told her you were a mystery writer, and she took it from there—the whole thing's a whopper dreamed up by a seasoned bullshitter."

"A whopper."

"Yeah."

"That's some imagination she's got then. Especially dreaming up that one-eyed apparition I clobbered."

"That was just her excuse to bullshit ya. Her starting point. That's probably something else, out of her real past, something her own fault, something less sensational. Maybe he's her boyfriend—or maybe her pimp!"

"Not her," I said, draining my beer. "Not a chance. She was no hooker. It was the truth—it was all there. In her face."

"Really got under your skin, didn't she?"

I ignored that, got up and went over to my turntable and turned the record over. When I came back and got settled on the couch again, I said, "Seems to me we're due for a change of subject again. So what the hell's been happening with you in the last couple of years?"

The next few hours went fast, and talk of old (and new) times almost pushed Janet and her fantastic story out of my head. But she was there, occupying a small corner of my mind, sitting patiently, silently, just as she had in the bus station.

I was turning on the television so John and I could catch the ten o'clock news when the phone rang. Thinking it might be Janet, I jumped for it.

"Yes?" I said.

"This is Brennan. Where the hell's my son?"

Brennan. Damn.

"Sorry, Sheriff," I said. "Been hogging him, haven't I? We got to drinking beer and talking, you know how it is."

"Put him on."

"Okay, okay, keep your badge on." I looked over at John. "He sounds even more belligerent than usual."

John took the phone and said hello and listened for a while and said yeah a few times and hung up.

"What's the deal?"

"Been an accident or something out on Colorado Hill. Says if I want to see him tonight I probably ought to forget it—he'll be tied up with this."

"Did he sound pissed off?"

"Yeah. He figures I should've stopped in to see him first."

"You should've."

"Why don't we drive out there and keep him company?"

"Won't we be a bother?"

"What? An Army sergeant and an ex-cop?"

"Well, okay," I said, "it's your home-coming. You got a right to spend it any crazy damn way you want. Let's go."

FIVE

There are two paved highways leading from Port City to Davenport, and Colorado Hill is on the older, less traveled of the two, a narrow strip of deteriorating concrete winding along the Mississippi. The only advantage of the older road—called by locals the River Road—is its scenery: Colorado Hill, for example. Since the Hill is only ten miles from Port City, most sightseers drive out there, sightsee, and turn back, not even thinking of using the River Road as a route to the nearby Quad Cities, though it remains well-traveled because of various factories and a stone quarry located along it.

"Damn," John said, working his voice up over the noise the Rambler made as it chugged along. "No moon, wouldn't you know it?"

"Dark night like this doesn't do much for the scenery *or* the driving." I was hunched forward, clutching the wheel, peeling my eyes for stray chunks of concrete, potholes and any bridges that might be out.

"I always liked this drive," John said. "I was looking forward to the view of the river."

"Try it on foot next time. At noon."

"Something up ahead, Mal."

"Yeah, I see it."

A quarter mile up two small dots of brightness were moving along either side of the road. As I neared them, the dots became flares, shooting off red-orange light, their bearers a couple teenage boys. I watched the boys set their flares to the left and right of the road and waited as one came running up to the car on my side; I rolled the window down and listened to him.

"Accident ahead! Accident ahead! You better turn back."

I nodded to the kid and rolled the window back up and crawled forward. In another fifty yards we came to a man setting another pair of flares, bigger ones, and he held out his palm for me to stop.

"Yeah?" I said.

It was Oliver DeForest, a guy who worked in a shoe store downtown, one of the Sheriff's Patrol—a group of citizens who

car, digging my hands down in my pockets, hunching my shoulders together, listening to my teeth chatter in my head. I stood among the trees that circled the open area, trees standing 'round like old women with tall thick bodies that for icy instants became their own long, cartoonish, wrinkled faces, with hair of skeletal branches that reached into the sky like dark seaweed, hanging upward.

They were having trouble getting the door pried open, so I went to help. Above us the sound of an ambulance's siren cut the air, distant and remote as a weak radio signal, but growing; the ledge up there where we'd been a few minutes ago cast an orange blush against the darkness. The door finally gave, and the smell of alcohol crawled out.

An empty bottle of Haig and Haig rested on the floor on the rider's side in the front, unbroken, the sole ironic survivor of the trip. The driver was not so lucky; a young blond woman crushed against and into the steel and glass of the smashed auto, a limp rag doll barely containing her stuffing, with the doll-face turned toward us, pretty much intact, eyes mercifully closed.

"Christ," I said, and covered my mouth, trying not to heave. I leaned against the wreckage and looked away. Looked out toward where the river was supposed to be, but through the trees and blackness I could see nothing, though the presence of the river was there, in the soft but distinct sounds of waves lapping, lapping.

Brennan snorted, disgusted by my reaction. "Seen a hell of a lot worse," he said.

"So has he," John said. "What is it, Mal?"

"The woman. In the car."

"What? Who? Somebody you know ...?"

"Somebody I just met."

"Christ," John said, understanding, and covered his mouth, and looked away.

PART TWO

NOVEMBER 27, 1974

WEDNESDAY

SIX

"So you told Brennan all of it," John said.

"That's right."

"The bruiser at the bus station, Janet Taber's story about the burning house, everything."

"Yup."

"And he just sat there. Didn't say a thing."

"Oh, he said something. He said, 'Why don't you go write one of your silly stories and leave me alone?'"

John was sitting across the table from me, wearing a blindingly orange turtleneck ski sweater. It was too early in the day to look at that sweater. John and I were upstairs in Brennan's living quarters over the jail, a study in drab browns except for the yellow kitchen the two of us were sitting in. It was nine o'clock, give or take a few minutes; I'd waited till this morning to tell my story to Brennan, downstairs in his office—last night at the accident scene, things had been too harried for that.

"Didn't he say at all what he's going to do about it?" John spoke through a bite of the eggs and potatoes I'd stood and watched him cook for himself minutes before.

"Nope," I said. "He'll talk to the coroner and arrange an autopsy, I suppose."

"Wait a minute, wait a minute. I can't picture this. He sat there and listened to that whole intricate story of yours, and then told you to get the hell out?"

"He wasn't as polite as all that."

"All 'round great guy, my stepdad."

"I wasn't supposed to come up here and wake you up, either. He'd like to 'see the boy get rested up,' you know."

"Hell with it. I don't know why I'm even staying here with him. If I had any sense I'd be over at my sister's."

"Sometimes I think Brennan doesn't like me."

"Perceptive. Very perceptive of you." John got up and took his dishes over to the sink and dumped them in, ran water over them. It was a somewhat strange sight, as the window over the sink, the only window in this typical American kitchen, was barred and caged. He turned to the icebox and got

out a jug of orange juice and asked if I
wanted some and I nodded.

He poured me some juice and said,
"How'd he react when he found out that
phone call you made from the depot yesterday wasn't a practical joke? That you
really *did* have a hassle with a big black
dude?"

"Like he reacted to everything else I told
him. Like I'd said, 'Nice day.' He muttered
something about never hearing of anybody
around here who fit that description."

"What about Janet Taber's mother? Has
he checked with Iowa City yet to see how
the old lady's doing?"

"Not yet he hasn't. I assume he's going
to. I suggested it, anyway."

"Mal."

"What?"

"You aren't satisfied, are you?"

"What's that supposed to mean?"

"You know what I mean. You aren't
satisfied you've gone and done your duty.
Paid off the obligation you feel you owe
that girl on the basis of the five-minute
relationship you had going with her."

I sipped the juice. I was starting to feel
awake; I could tell because my eyes could
focus on John's bright orange sweater without fuzzing up on me.

I said, "No."

"No, what?"

"No, I'm not satisfied."

"All right. You're not satisfied. Where do you go from here? I'm not auditioning to play Tonto to your Lone Ranger, understand—I'm just interested."

"Well." I took another sip of the juice. "This is how I figure it. I got a few days off now for Thanksgiving. Don't have to register for new classes at the college till Tuesday. That gives me almost a week to do some nosing around."

"What is this, research? So you've sold a few mystery stories. That doesn't make you a . . . a private eye, you know. That's a fantasy, Mal."

"Give me a little credit, John. I'm just going to ask a few questions. If I turn something up, something your stepdad can't ignore, I'll toss him the ball, I promise."

He shook his head. "Mal, I lost my father—my real father—a long time ago; and Mom not so long ago. You lost your folks. We both saw friends die, in the war. People dying is a thing we've both faced. Had to face."

"Yes. That's true."

"So you know as well as I do that there's no way to make the dead rest easier. Nobody'll rest easier, Mal. Nobody."

"I'll rest easier."

He thought about that; then something went across his face that meant he'd made some sort of decision. He leaned forward with an intense, knit-brow look and said,

"Now don't go getting excited or anything . . ."

"What? What are you . . . ?"

"It's maybe nothing. It's something I'm not at all sure about, understand. It was dark last night and I was tired and I was full of beer."

"What are you getting at, John?"

"I think I maybe knew that girl."

"Janet, you mean? You knew Janet?"

"I'm not sure, Mal."

"Why the hell didn't you tell me this last night?"

"I wasn't sure, I said, and you were flaky enough as it was. It was just too far-fetched. I thought it was just power of suggestion, you know, you mention the name Janet and I subconsciously confuse her with a Janet I knew once."

"Who the hell *was* this Janet you knew?"

"Just a friend of my sister's, back when I was still in high school."

"High school. Should I have known her?"

"No, this was after you graduated. You were a year ahead of me, remember."

"No, hold on, this is impossible. My Janet lived in Des Moines. She only moved to Port City within the last few months."

"That's just it, Mal. My Janet lived in Des Moines. She was only in Port City for one summer."

"How did your sister know her?"

"They worked together, at some summer job. I don't remember what."

"Christ, her last name, what was her last name, can you remember that?"

"Uh . . . Ferris, I think. I think her name was Janet Ferris."

I sighed. I drained my glass of orange juice and poured another out of the jug. I was awake. "That clinches it then. You *were* just imagining things. My Janet's last name was Taber."

"Maybe that was her married name."

"Don't think so. This guy she lived with, it was just a common-law thing, I don't figure she ever took his name. I . . ."

The clomp of footsteps in the hall cut in, announcing that the head of the house was on his way for a visit. Moments later Brennan's bulky frame filled the kitchen doorway, and he said, "What the hell are you doing here, Mallory? I thought I told you to leave the boy sleep."

"I was up, sir," John said.

"Well, okay."

I said, "What'd you find out?"

Brennan gave me his slow look, tension tightening his jaw muscles; he was getting ready to have another go at me, but John stopped him.

"Why are you coming down so hard on Mal, when he's just trying to help you out?" John asked him, dropping the "sir" as though it had just occurred to him that Brennan wasn't his commanding officer.

But Brennan ignored John and held his gaze on me. He was trying to keep an expression of control, of confidence on his face, but it wasn't working out for him.

Finally he said, "Before you ask me any more questions, Mallory, I got something to lay on you: just keep your damn butt out of my business. And this whole deal is *my business*. You had some information, you delivered it, now go on home, damn it. Shoo."

And I said, "I'm not a bystander, Brennan. Whether you like it or not, I'm an active participant. If you find any evidence of foul play, I'll be a top prosecution witness, you know. So be nice to me, Brennan. Satisfy the curiosity of this concerned citizen."

He came over and sat down at the table with us, changed his expression to one that was about as friendly as he could muster for me. Sort of a warm grimace.

He said, "I appreciate you letting me know about the circumstances surrounding that accident last night. I really do. I'm obliged to you for that much, don't get me wrong."

"Then tell me about the autopsy."

He started to get mad all over again, then sighed in momentary defeat. "We're trying to contact next of kin. After a reasonable attempt's been made, we can go on ahead with it."

John said. "What about the girl's mother?"

Brennan shook his head. "Called the University Hospital just before I came up here. Old lady Ferris is out of the picture."

"Who?" I said.

"The mother," Brennan said. "Renata Ferris, age fifty-nine. She died around four this morning."

SEVEN

John's sister Lori and her husband and newborn child lived in a duplex on East Hill, just a few blocks from my trailer—the lower floor of a paint-peeling gothic two-story.

When John knocked, we heard "Come on in," and did, finding Lori sitting on the couch, with her blouse unbuttoned, holding her baby to one beautiful, mostly exposed breast. She apologized for not rising. Lori is a pretty, shapely little thing, with long brown hair highlighted with red, and milky white skin freckled here and there. Her breasts, judging from the one that was showing, were pale ivory, and let me state now that watching a beautiful woman breast-feed a child is something I'll never get used to, and not just because I was a bottle baby myself.

Lori and John had a lot to talk about, so I kept fairly quiet for the first half hour. They hadn't seen each other since his emergency leave when their mother died, which had been just before he left for his second tour in Vietnam. John didn't say much about his overseas duty, but he did have a few words to say, mostly bitter, about California and the wife he'd briefly had out there. Lori told John that her husband Frank wasn't in a rock group anymore, but was playing four evenings a week in a local bar with a country-western band, which was helping to supplement the salary from his job at the alcohol plant. She was going to try to stay at home with the child, Jeff, and hoped she wouldn't have to go back to secretarial work.

Finally I said, "Lori, I wonder if you'd mind if I butt in for a moment."

Her brown eyes flashed sexily, an unsettling thing for a mother breast-feeding her child to do (unsettling for me, that is), and she said, "Not at all, Mal."

"John told me this morning that you used to know a girl named Janet Ferris."

Lori nodded. "I still do. I mean, we're not real close, but I know her."

John and I exchanged glances.

"And," she said, "her name isn't Ferris anymore. She got married to a guy named

Phil Taber. They're split up but she's still using the name."

"Have you seen her lately?"

"Sure. Last week. She moved back to Port City several months ago."

John said, "You better tell her, Mal."

Lori shifted the child from one breast to the other. "Tell me what?"

I said, "Janet Taber was killed last night."

"God, no! But . . . how? What happened?"

John said, "A car crash."

"An accident?"

"That's what it looks like," I said. "But I think there's a chance it was something else."

"God," Lori said. "And after all she's been through." She shook her head. "I wonder what'll happen to her boy. That freaky husband of hers won't take care of him. The kid's in bad shape, you know. Very bad shape."

"How bad?"

"Bad shape like in open heart surgery."

John said, "The appearance of the accident was that Janet was drunk at the wheel and went over the side out at Colorado Hill."

"That's a load of bull," Lori said. "Booze made Janet nauseous—she couldn't stand the stuff! I've seen her smoke a joint now and then, but hard liquor? No way."

"Well," I said.

Lori eased her child away from her

breast and rose up from the couch, saying, "Excuse me." Several minutes later, having tucked the baby away in his crib, she came back, buttoning her white blouse.

"What's your interest in Janet, Mal?" Lori said, sadly, sitting back down on the couch. "I didn't realize Janet and I shared a mutual friend in you. She never mentioned you."

I told her the story. I'd been through the bus station incident so many times I was beginning to feel prerecorded. Lori leaned forward, intent on my words, the intelligence sharp in her brown eyes. When I finished up, she said, "Wow," and shook her head. "Some story."

"And," I said, "since I'm on Thanksgiving vacation . . ."

"Don't mention the word Thanksgiving," she said. "I've been wrestling with a turkey all morning. I'll be glad when tomorrow's out of the way. I'm having Brennan and John over and . . ."

John interrupted. "Mal's not changing the subject to his holiday plans, sis. He's really caught up in this Janet Taber thing. He wants to do something about it."

"The only thing to do," Lori said, "is fill Brennan in on it. He's a little right-wing, I'll grant you, but then Port County is the most Republican county in this Republican state. Brennan's a good sheriff—don't let his redneck attitude fool you."

"I just came from talking to Brennan," I said. "And I came away with the feeling he doesn't really take this too seriously."

"Why not?"

"Maybe because I'm involved. I don't know."

"So what are you gonna do? Play cop?"

"I was one once, you know."

Lori smirked. "Yeah, you rode around in a squad car out in some California equivalent of Port City for what, a month and a half before you quit? Big deal."

"Lori," John said.

"Look, Mal," she said, "I like you and all that, but I'm not in favor of helping out anybody who's got in mind taking the law in his own hands. I'm an *ex*-radical these days, all settled down and married and a mother, and I'm for working through the system, not running over it."

"Don't pay any attention to her," John told me, "she's been a schizophrenic for years, trying to be a left-wing antiwar liberal on the one hand, and supporting that super-conservative stepfather sheriff of ours on the other."

"Lori," I said, "I just want to poke around a little bit and see if I can uncover some truth. Is there anything wrong with that?"

Her expression froze in an undecided half-smile, and she sat back and thought it over for a while. John started to coax her, but I waved at him to shut up.

Finally she sighed and started pouring out everything she knew about Janet Ferris Taber.

"Five years ago," she said, "when I was a student at the Community College, I had this summer job, a job I felt would be rewarding in more ways than just financial. The job was being a full-time secretary on the campaign team for U.S. Senate hopeful Richard Norman."

"Norman, huh?"

"Yeah. Norman, our local wonder boy."

Son of Port City's resident eccentric millionaire, Sy Norman, young Norman had been a top honors man in college and a letter-winner in track to boot, and had gone on to be first in his class in the University law school. His next achievement was being the youngest man in the state's history to be elected to the Iowa legislature. He served his district well (which included his home town, Port City, of course) for ten years, then began to mount his campaign to reach Washington.

"I was eager to help him," she said. "I'd been vice-president of the Young Demos at the college and Norman was a Republican. But, he was a liberal Republican, and that was about as far to the left as this state could ever be expected to move, so I jumped in with both idealistic feet.

"The other full-time secretary on the campaign team was Janet Ferris, a young student the same age as me who went to Drake in Des Moines, and in her spare time during the school year'd worked as a part-time secretary in Norman's office, in the Capitol Building. Norman had brought Janet from Des Moines to Port City, which was to be the launching pad for his campaign. She and I became close friends, worked intimately together, shared the same dedication to Norman—Janet always spoke of the senator in glowing terms—and the summer months went quickly by.

"Janet and I had our tearful good-byes at the bus station, Janet heading back for Des Moines and Norman, to help him continue with phase two of his campaign, and me back to the Community College and part-time work on the local level as a Norman Volunteer.

"On the whole," she said, "even though we were college students, Janet and I had a very high school-ish relationship. Giggling girls caught up in the importance of what we were doing—you know, helping to change the world and all. When we got together last month, after I found out she was back in town, it was an awkward situation. I mean, we were 'friends' with a relationship based on something past, and everything that happened to her since I saw her last was such a downer. We never did say much about that summer we worked for Norman. Sometimes I wonder how Janet must've taken it when Norman lost."

"Norman," I said.

"Whatever happened to him?" John asked.

"Norman's dead," I said. "He and his family were killed in some freak accident, as I recall."

Lori nodded. "A sad thing. He was getting ready to make another bid, this time for the House, and the polls had him out front, too."

"He's dead?" John said.

"Yes," Lori said. "A car crash, two or three years ago or so. He and his wife and little girl. Say, you know something funny . . . now isn't that strange."

"What?" John said.

"The crash he was in," she said. She paused. "Seems to me *that* happened out on . . ."

"Out on Colorado Hill," I said.

EIGHT

I opened the Rambler door with my free hand and struggled with the other to balance a wobbly cardboard tray, the tray trying desperately to contain its cargo of one fat white paper bag and two lidded paper cups. I handed the tray in to John and let him juggle with it for a while, amazed at the ease with which he set it safely down on the seat between us, and watched as he drew out two hamburgers and a little sack of french fries from the bag, leaving in it the same configuration of food for me. My Rambler was one of many cars squeezed into the lot at Sandy's for noontime conversion into dining rooms.

"Mal," John said, unwrapping one of his hamburgers, "about both those accidents being out at Colorado Hill . . ."

"Yeah?"

"That could be a legitimate coincidence, you know. Don't rule it out, anyway. Hardly a year goes by without one or two accidents out there."

I nodded.

A minute or so went by, the sound in the car one of mouths chewing, not talking. In between hamburgers, John said, "Mal?"

"What?"

"You going to keep snooping around today?"

"Planned to."

"Well, uh . . ."

"Well, uh, what?"

"You suppose you could drop me off some place after we eat?"

"Sure. Any place in particular?"

"Suzie Blanchard's. It's over on Spring."

"Suzie Blanchard? Well, some things never change, I guess. But isn't she married?"

"Divorced."

"She expecting you?"

"No. I'd kind of like to surprise her."

"I'll bet. I didn't know you two had kept in touch."

"Just the last few months or so—we've been writing letters."

"I see. Will she be home? Doesn't she have a job?"

"No, she's got a kid. By-product of the marriage."

"Oh. Well. You won't want me around."

"Right."

I started in on my french fries.

John said. "What are you going to do this afternoon?"

"Thought I'd run over to the college and see Jack Masters. I figure if anybody in town can give me a line on that black guy at the bus station, it'll be Jack."

"Not a bad idea, Mal. Mal?"

"Yeah?"

"You won't mind it, me dropping out of the picture for a while?"

"No, no."

"I'll stop by your trailer around eight, okay? And see how it's going."

"Sure. And if you get stranded anywhere, just call me and I'll play taxi."

"You sure you don't mind?"

"Not at all. This is *my* hang-up, not yours."

"I can probably help you out later on."

"Sure. When I uncover a vast Communist conspiracy behind all this, I'll just about have to send for the Marines, won't I?"

He grinned. "That's Army, kid. Keep it straight."

I grinned back and started peeling away the wrapper from the second hamburger. "Suzie Blanchard, huh?"

"Man does not live by french fry alone," John said, biting into one.

*   *   *

Down the right half of the hall, on the left side, was the college office, and beyond the glass wall of the outer office all the typewriters were covered and desks cleared and employees gone, except for Jack Masters, of course, who was in one of the inner offices with the door open, talking on his phone. It was Thanksgiving vacation and the Community College was otherwise empty.

I took a seat in the outer office and sat watching Jack bark at the superintendent over his phone.

It reminded me of the day a couple months back when our conservative, near-elderly dean was showing a bunch of guys from the North Central accrediting board around the school, and when they went into Jack's office, he was wearing a Hamm's Beer sweat shirt and smoking a cigar, his feet on his desk. The dean blew what of his lid was left after many such confrontations with Jack, but the North Central boys said nothing, sensing the rapport Jack had built with the two young men he was in the process of counseling.

Jack is five-eight, and near as wide as he is tall, though he isn't fat. He's chunky, and he's got a paunch, but he isn't fat. His age is indeterminate: he could be forty, he could be fifty. He looks more like a truck driver than a Dean of Admissions of a college, and he's black.

Jack was a token black who backfired profoundly on his employers. Besides championing liberal causes and pushing his own and other minorities down the throats of an unwilling school board, Jack didn't play by the unspoken rules. For instance, there was the case of the woman he was living with—a white woman. She had an apartment downtown over one of Port City's many taverns, and unofficial word came from the school board that the Dean of Admissions shouldn't be seen coming in and out of the apartment of such a woman ("such" being a euphemism for "white," one supposes). Jack said, well, fine, then he'd be glad to marry the gal and make it legal. No further criticism of the Dean of Admissions's love life was heard.

I watched as he hung up the phone. He spotted me waiting and grinned and waved me in.

"You got a minute, Jack?"

"Sure, Mallory, sure." He gestured to the chair opposite his desk. He didn't have his Hamm's shirt on this time, just an off-white sport shirt.

I sat down. "Been going a few rounds with the superintendent?"

"Naturally." He offered me a cigarette and I declined while he lit one up. "From major issues to minor. Like, he thinks the Ag boys should be excused from the Humanities, but I think they need a history course, not just history of the plow, and a literature course, not just 'How to Read a Harvester Manual.' And then there's that black kid from Moline he wants expelled, just because the kid called his gym instructor a mother."

I laughed. "Sounds like a term of endearment to me."

He shook his head, smiled. Slapped his desk. "Well, what can I do for you, Mallory? You don't need *counseling*, for Christ's sake."

"I need some information. And it's nothing to do with school."

"What is it, then?"

It was something like the hundredth time I'd gone through the story, but if it seemed stale to me, it didn't to Jack: he leaned forward, intense interest on his walnut-stained face.

When I finished, Jack leaned back and said, "So what now? What're you going to do? Investigate? You're no detective."

"I know that. But all I'm going to do is ask some questions, do a little research. If I can come up with anything really concrete, I'll turn it over to Brennan."

"Why not leave it to him *now?*"

"I didn't think you thought much of Brennan, Jack."

"I don't. But in the context of this town, he's a pretty good man. Port City's sheriff has to be a little lazy and a little corrupt if he's going to be an accurate reflection of his town. But when the need arises, Brennan pulls himself up to it."

I nodded. "Well, then, you can see why I'm going to have to come up with something solid, something Brennan can't ignore, if I'm to possibly get him up off his can."

Jack shrugged. "All well and good, but I still can't give you my approval of what you're up to."

"I don't want your approval. Just some help. And I think you know in what way you can help me."

"Sure. The big black guy with one eye you tangled with."

"Do you know him?"

"Maybe. I'll go even so far as to say probably. After all, there can't be too many six-four, one-eyed blacks around these parts. But it surprises me to hear of this, for two reasons. First, I haven't seen him around in maybe a year. And second, he was an okay guy, I'd almost say he was a gentleman."

"Take my word for it, he wasn't gentle. How do you know him? You know his name?"

"His name is Washington. I don't know if it's his first or last. I've heard him called Eyewash, by his close friends. I used to run into him up in the Quad Cities, Davenport mostly, in any of three or four bars,

bars catering to blacks, or to blacks and whites who wish to mix."

"You still hit those clubs?"

"Once in a while. Since they moved me up from Sociology prof to desk jockey, I've had more responsibility on my hands than free time. I still make the rounds of the bars once a month or so, and I haven't run into Washington in a year at least."

"In spite of that, it does sound like the same guy."

"Probably is. But if he's moved from the Cities to somewhere else, it isn't Port City, or we'd both know about it. He isn't the kind of guy you don't notice."

"Anything else you can think of about him?"

"Yeah, he's got a sister. I'm not talking soul sister, either, an honest-to-God blood sister. Rita, her name is. Very nice."

"That so?"

"Pretty thing. Younger than her brother. 'Round twenty-five or so. I've seen her around some."

"Lately?"

"Yeah, last time I was up there. She's still around."

"Maybe I can track her down and find Washington through her."

"Could be."

"How'd he lose the eye? He ever mention it?"

"I hear he lost it in a gang fight, when

he was a kid. He came from Chicago originally. South Side."

"Thought you said he was gentle."

"Far as I know, he is. Always nice to the ladies. Saw him back down from a few fights, too. Big guy like him always has challengers, you know, and he'd just ignore any flack."

"What does he do for a living?"

"I got no idea. He dressed well, but most of the brothers—all but me, anyway—dress to the teeth." He got out a piece of paper and scribbled down several lines. "Here's the names and addresses of a couple clubs you can try, to run down his sister. But Mallory . . ."

"Yes, Jack?"

"Watch your lily-white ass."

I grinned. "At all times."

He leaned back again, stabbing out his cigarette in a tray. "You know, though . . . if I were you I'd try a safer approach."

"Such as?"

"Explore that Norman character. Both the old man and the son. Check it out before you go any further and see if it's just a coincidence, this Colorado Hill thing."

"I might just do that."

"It ought to be fun, researching the old man. Simon Harrison Norman. Hell of a character."

"Oh?"

"Sure, hell, didn't you ever hear about how he raised his fortune?"

"Something to do with patent medicine, wasn't it?"

"I'll say! It's one of Port City's few lasting claims to fame. Sy Norman, back in the thirties, was the country's leading cancer quack. Sold mineral water in a bottle as a cancer cure. Made a pile. Rumor has it he's a silent partner back of the five major industries in this town. Look it all up. It'll be good reading, if nothing else."

NINE

I was hunched over, staring into the microfilm viewer at the city library, turning the crank that caused day after day of *Port City Journal*s to glide across my vision. I'd started with January three years past, had gone through the first roll, which took me to April, and was now on the second, just into May. I was half-hypnotized by the filmed pages as they swam across my path of sight, but was shaken awake by a screaming headline: SENATOR NORMAN DIES IN CRASH. A smaller, unintentionally ambiguous headline above said WIFE AND CHILD CRITICAL.

A studio photograph of Norman, his wife and daughter, taken only a month before, was on one side of the single column story that ran down the center of the page. On the other side was a long shot of the precipice at Colorado Hill where the Norman car had gone over. The picture showed Sheriff Brennan standing at the edge, looking down over the dropoff, much as he'd been last night when John and I approached him.

According to the *Journal* account, the Norman family had been on the way home after spending an evening with friends in Davenport. The night had been a particularly dark one, no moon, and the senator apparently had "simply misjudged" the curve at the Hill. The account said the senator had not been speeding, and that the senator had not been drinking. This denial raised the questions it sought to suppress.

I spun the manual control on the machine and eased the next day's front page into view. Reported there was the death of Norman's wife, and both Mr. and Mrs. Norman's obituaries; printing an obituary on the front page is (speaking as an ex-newspaperman) the highest honor a paper can pay a corpse. From Norman's obit I learned nothing John's sister Lori hadn't already told me. I kept turning. Two *Journal*s later I read of the young daughter's death. Her obit was shortest and saddest.

I got up from the machine and went over to the desk where Brenda Halwin was working. Brenda is a nicely built, pretty blonde, a year ahead of me at the college, four years behind me in age. The sight and company of her could cheer me up after almost anything, and I hoped this would be no exception.

"Finished?" Brenda asked.

"I'm not sure. For right now, maybe. How far back do these microfilmed *Journal*s go?" I'd never gone back past the early forties.

"Very far. Seventy years, I think."

I thought about asking Brenda what she was doing tonight. I thought about the night two weeks ago when Brenda had been with me at my trailer. I thought about another blonde, almost as pretty, but with roots, and dead.

I said, "I guess you better pull out the thirties drawer for me, Brenda."

I wasn't cheered up; it wasn't like I hadn't tried to be. I just wasn't.

Brenda started me with January, 1930, and half an hour later I was beginning January, 1931, and had yet to see the name Simon Harrison Norman in print.

"Reading the old comic strips again, Mr. Mallory?"

I looked up from the machine. It was Miss Simmons, an elderly, attractive lady who'd been head librarian for as long as I could remember. She was the kind of "old

maid" who makes it difficult to understand how she got that way; in Miss
Simmons's case, so gossip went, her true
love had died in the Great War. Whichever
war that was.

"Frankly, Miss Simmons," I said, "I'm
trying to avoid the comics, though I find
them and the old movie ads tempting. I've
got more serious research on my mind."

"What subject, Mr. Mallory?"

"A local recluse of sorts. Rich recluse.
Simon Norman."

"Ah, Mr. Norman." She smiled a small,
mysterious smile, a smile out of a Gothic
novel, and said, "Quite a personality, our
Mr. Norman. But you won't find much of
him in the pages of the *Port City Journal*."

"Oh?"

"That is, outside of, perhaps, a scathing
editorial or two."

"Why's that?"

"Mr. Norman was competition. He was
publisher and editor of his *own* daily newspaper, the *Midwest Clarion*, which gave the
Journal a run for the money. The *Journal*
saw fit to exclude coverage of Mr. Norman
in their pages."

"No kidding," I said. I looked at the
microfilm machine and the box of spools
beside it. "But it does present a problem
for me."

"Yes, of course. And for a long time now,

Mr. Norman has displayed a distinct dislike for publicity, so recent write-ups are few and far between. You could check the *Reader's Guide* for national coverage, but our magazine collection of the thirties is quite limited."

"You wouldn't have microfilm files on the *Clarion*?"

"No. None have survived to be filmed."

"And nothing on him in recent years? What about during his son's political campaigns?"

"Well, there were some attempts to smear the Norman boy by dredging up his father's misdeeds. But such reports would hardly be objective. Besides, most of the newspapers in the state—the *Journal* and the *Register* included—supported young Norman and declined giving detailed accounts of the speeches that included such smears."

"Well."

"You seem disturbed, Mr. Mallory. More disturbed than problems with a research paper might warrant."

"This isn't a research paper I'm working on. This is something more important than that."

She thought for a moment, then said, "I think I can help you." She turned away and disappeared into her office.

Five minutes later, while I was standing flirting with Brenda, Miss Simmons came up to us, gave her employee a sharp look that was mostly pretense, and handed me a small, square magazine. The magazine was marked with a white shard of paper.

"If you can tear yourself away from Miss Halwin," Miss Simmons said, "and rekindle your enthusiasm for research, this should prove sufficient."

I did, and it did.

TEN

The magazine was called *The Periodical of Iowa History*, was dated four years ago, and in an article called "Port City's Millionaire Cancer Quack," had this to say:

Port City has had more than its quota of controversial citizens during its century-and-a-half history.

One local character spread his controversial nature nationwide: Simon Harrison Norman, "Doc Sy," operator of a "cancer clinic" in Port City. Norman lives there to this day, in a seclusion markedly contrasting his days as a flamboyant con man, when he drove around the state of Iowa in his purple Cadillac and matching color shirt.

"Doc Sy" was not a doctor, of course

. . . he didn't even make it out of the eighth grade. But higher education was no barrier for Simon Harrison Norman.

Cancer is Cured

By a skillful if crude manipulation of mass media, Norman drew thousands of the despairing and desperate to Port City in the early thirties, with his slogan "Cancer is Cured" as a lure.

He printed his magazine *TKO* (Truth Kills Obstacles) and operated radio station KTKO, using Port City as his base. According to his magazine, "Doctor Norman has proven beyond any doubt that even the worst, so-called 'terminal' case of cancer can be cured." Open air meetings, attended by as many as 40,000 persons (five times the size of Port City at the time), watched the showman Norman, an ex-stage hypnotist, perform his miracles.

His purple Cadillac and purple shirt became trademarks of Norman's when he moved his rallies to towns all through Iowa, touching at times Illinois, Nebraska and Wisconsin.

Such activities brought money in by the barrelsful. The "clinic" reaped profits of $50,000 a month by 1932, and Norman boasted around that time that his "personal consultations" netted him $30,000 on an average week. That these profits were plucked from desolate, poverty-torn Depression families mattered not to Norman. Asked in 1934 by a Des Moines *Register* reporter how he (Norman) could live with himself after victimizing destitute families, Doc Sy said, "There are no 'victims' at the Norman Clinic—only cured, healthy patients, ready to embark on a new life—which my staff and I have given them."

Norman "gave" nothing—one fifteen-year-old Waterloo boy in later years reported paying Norman's $100-a-week fee for the "treatment" of his father; comparable rates in a reputable hospital of the era, staffed by physicians, would be around $30 a week. The father, of course, died, in spite of Norman's treatments and injections. One man used by Norman in a radio broadcast as "living proof of our miraculous cures" died within a month. The man's wife later said that they had paid $300 for the cure, against the advice of their family doctor, who told them the case was without hope.

A photo story in *TKO* called "Ten 'New' Men," reporting on a number of "successful" Norman patients, included two who didn't live long enough to see the article reach print.

Quack King

When an American Medical Association spokesman said, "Of all the heartless, vicious ghouls preying on the dead and those who are about to die, Simon Norman is quack king," Norman took it as a compliment. Over the door of his clinic he hung a sign saying, "Docs quack—Quacks cure."

Norman guarded the secret of his "cure" very carefully, once saying, "A well-known doctor devised it for me, before his death," another time saying, "A traveler to the Himalayas passed it on to me before his untimely demise." (Norman apparently could cure neither of his benefactors.) Chemists of the day found the "secret" easily unlocked: one Norman concoction was made up of equal parts alcohol and glycerin, with a dab of peppermint oil; a second was nothing more than mineral oil; a third was red clover blossom syrup, which could be purchased in the early thirties for $2 a gallon. Ordinary facial powder served as treatment of external cancer.

Norman was born in Port City and

left in his mid-teens to take advantage of his tall, lean good looks—particularly the piercing gray eyes—by becoming a stage hypnotist. In the early twenties Norman was making calliopes on the side, selling them to the circuses, carnivals and riverboats in which he worked his stage act. By the late twenties he was a broadcaster, peddling clocks, brooms, coffee, underwear, flour, tires, furniture and silverware through the magic of radio.

Sometime around 1929, when the fortunes of others were quite low, Norman apparently ran into either the famous doctor or the Himalayan traveler, because by late that year he was on the air pitching his cancer cures. By early 1930, construction had begun on his clinic; by mid-1931, he cut the ribbon on his radio station; and, by early '33, had his own daily newspaper, the *Midwest Clarion*. President Herbert Hoover, himself a native Iowan from West Branch, had forged a golden key and sent it on to Norman for him to use to start the *Clarion* presses.

Short Reign

Norman's reign as quackery king was not as long as he would have liked, but it did last a full decade. By

1940, he was out of Port City, after several legal battles, and by 1942 began serving the four-year term in federal prison handed down in '41 by the courts.

It was the AMA and other medical societies whose unofficial declaration of war on Norman finally caused his downfall. Ironically, his own reaction to their jabs at him in the *AMA Journal* caused him more trouble than the AMA itself: Norman vented so much fury in his KTKO counterattacks that the Federal Communications Commission yanked his license.

Without his most important base of pitchmanship—the radio—Norman, swamped by countless lawsuits, moved his clinic to Hot Springs, Arkansas, adding their famous waters to his own "cures," and changed the name of his station to XTKO, the transmitter safely over the border in Mexico.

But less than a year later, his new set-up thriving, Norman was charged by the U.S. Government for using the mails to defraud, and by 1942 Doc Sy was in Leavenworth.

Remorseful Doc

In 1946 he returned to Iowa, sans purple shirt and purple car, and retired into seclusion. He has been there ever since, apparently doing nothing more than sitting around counting the reported one million dollars he racked up during his reign as king of quacks. All but forgotten by the press, even in the case of his son's political career, Norman's influence is said to continue via a string of Port City industries in which he is supposedly a silent partner.

Another rumor has it that Doc Sy picked up a strain of remorse during his ·stay at Leavenworth, and it is believed by some that he is the guiding light behind his well-known and respected son, Republican politico Richard Norman, who has been successful in Iowa politics, though failing in his bid to reach the U.S. Senate. The *Register* has called young Norman "the most socially concerned, dedicated young man in the state legislature," a sore point among Demos, who feel such areas their private domain. Assertions that Doc Sy's son is trying to atone for his father's misanthropy, or that the father is attempting to make amends to society through the deeds of his son, are pure speculation.

But it is a fact that the primary failure of Doc Sy's fabulous years as the quackery king was his own unsuccessful attempt to snatch the Republican nomination for U.S. Senate from an incumbent senator.

And yet another fact may be key in explaining the elder Norman's supposed attack of remorse: May Belle (Peterson) Norman, his wife and bearer of son Richard, died in 1945 . . . of lung cancer.

ELEVEN

Half an hour later I walked into the cluttered living room of my trailer, picking things up as I went and spending half an hour cleaning up the place—more as a nervous accompaniment to buzzing thoughts than as an act of cleanliness. When I was finished playing maid, I went to the icebox and got out a Pabst and popped the top and went back and flopped down on the couch. After I'd drained the beer, I aimed the empty can at the wastebasket over by the stove, across the room; just as I pitched the can, the phone rang, shattering my concentration, ruining my trajectory. The can clattered on the kitchenette's tile floor, bounced back onto the carpeted living room floor, rolled a couple times and came to a standstill somewhere near center-room, creating an eyesore in my freshly tidied quarters.

The phone was still ringing on the coffee table in front of me. I leaned over and picked up the receiver. "Yeah?"

"Mal? John."

"Oh, hi. How was Suzie Blanchard?"

"Outstanding."

"That's Army for 'good,' as I recall."

"At least."

"So what's up? No pun intended."

"That's what I called to ask you, Mal. What have you turned up where Janet Taber's concerned?"

"I did some research at the library on that politician Janet worked for, and on his old man. Did you know that that guy Doc Sy, the old cancer quack, was Richard Norman's father?"

"Come to think of it," John said, "that's right. You know, you don't hear much about the old man around town. Funny."

"Yeah. Funny. It's one of those things Port City folks just don't talk about. Unless the doors are closed tight. And I think I know why. I think the old ex-quack's still powerful in Port City inner circles."

"How do you figure?"

"Well, I can't really say for sure, I'm mostly reading between the lines. But it's beginning to look like Simon Norman is Port City's answer to Howard Hughes. One thing I know for sure is he made a bundle, and made it off of people's misery, at that. And he probably used that bundle to get behind a few budding concerns that developed into this town's major industries, which'd include the feed plant, the office furniture company, the alcohol plant, the tire retreading factory—all of these and more, I bet."

"How does this tie in with Janet Taber?"

"I don't know that it does."

I heard chattering in the background, and then John's voice came back: "Uh, look, I'm still over at Suzie's and, uh, I guess she wants a word with me."

"And I can just guess what word it is. Look, see if you can find time today, between rounds, to stop over at Brennan's and pump him a little."

"See what I can do. I'll stop over and see you tonight."

I cradled the receiver on my shoulder, thumbed down the button on the phone with one hand and fumbled through the phone book with the other, trying to locate the college's number. I found it and dialed. I got Jack and filled him in on my library session.

"You aren't thinking about trying to run down Washington's sister Rita tonight, are you?" Jack asked.

"I was thinking about it, yeah."

"I wouldn't."

"Why? I'm a big boy now."

"Not that big. With Thanksgiving tomorrow, the bars'll be extra busy tonight. You know how it is night before a holiday. It might get a little rough if you go sailing in a black bar with that shinin' white kisser of yours."

"Ah, hell with that, Jack. I got to do something, and soon. I hate this sitting on the thing like this. I want to move on it, and I got nowhere else to go with it, except the Quad Cities and Washington's sister, Rita."

"Why don't you just relax tonight—get your head together, son. Tell you want, I'll do some checking tonight and see what *I* can find out about old Eyewash and his sister."

"You don't have to do that, Jack."

"I insist."

"But . . ."

"Look, it's a terrific excuse for me to go bar crawlin', son. I'm due."

"Well, thanks. I'll check back with you tomorrow morning."

"Late morning. Gimme a break. Hey, what'd you turn up on Stefan Norman?"

"Who?"

"Stefan Norman. Did you try to contact him or anything?"

"I never even *heard* of him. Which Norman is *he?*"

"He's the nephew of the old man. Norman's late brother's boy."

"How does he fit into the Norman empire, Jack?"

"Well, the Norman empire, if there is one, appears to operate on a hereditary basis, only the ruling class has just about died out. You probably found out this afternoon that Norman's wife died of cancer back in the forties, and son Richard's dead, of course . . . and Richard was Norman's only child. Norman has no brothers or sisters living—only had the one brother, and his only child was Stefan. Who is heir to the Norman empire, such as it is."

"What role does this Stefan play in Norman's life, as of now?"

"He's in charge of something called the Norman Fund, has been ever since Richard died. Of course, he was pretty much in charge before that, too, since Richard was only a figurehead 'chairman' for the Fund; he had his political career, and his law practice as well."

"What the hell's the Norman Fund, anyway?"

"I don't know, but I got a feeling if you could find out, the two of us could blackmail old man Norman and God knows who else and live comfortably for the rest of our lives off the proceeds. I suppose it's a clearing house for the different under-the-table ties Norman has with the various industries in town. It plays at being a charitable organization. But all I can speak of for certain is the physical reality of a three-office suite here in town, in the Maxwell Building."

"I wish I'd known about this this afternoon. . . ."

"I forget that some of this stuff that's common knowledge to me, from the business types I come in contact with, is news to you. I should've mentioned it. Sorry."

"That's okay. But I've got to see this Stefan Norman. He sounds like the man who could once and for all fill me in on how much—or how little—Janet Taber had to do with the Normans. The Maxwell Building, you said? Think anyone would be in the office now?"

"No way. It's after five."

"Damn. Stefan Norman live in Port City?"

"No. Davenport, I believe. Commutes down every day, I assume."

"Well, sooner or later I'll have to take a little drive up to the Quad Cities and see these people."

"Make it later. I'll handle this Washington thing for you tonight, and by myself. The first round of it, anyway."

He hung up and so did I. I leaned back on the couch.

Next thing I knew, John was bursting in the door.

"Jesus Christ," I said. "Why not give me a goddamn heart attack while you're at it?"

"Never mind that," he said. He threw his coat off and sat down near me on the couch. I glanced at my watch: I didn't remember falling asleep, but I sure had, because it was almost nine P.M., now.

He said, "I went over to the jail for a few minutes and pumped Brennan, like you said, and I got some choice items for you. First off, they had the autopsy. Janet's neck was broken, all right, and there was some discussion involving the fact that it could have been caused by a pair of strong hands, 'cause of the bruises and all, but in light of the crash's impact, that's hard to say. The final judgment was that she died in the crash, but get this ... there was no alcohol in her bloodstream!"

I felt a smile work its way across my face.

"I asked him who okayed the autopsy," he said, "and he told me no immediate member of the family was available, so with the court's permission the hospital boys went ahead with it. But that's bull-shit." He dug in his pocket for a moment, came up with a scrap of paper. "You think *you've* been playing detective? Dig this. You ever see in the movies or on TV where if somebody writes on a notepad, you can rub a pencil edge across the under-sheet and make out what was written on the sheet torn off?"

I nodded.

"Well, upstairs by the phone there's a notepad. And I decided to check up on Brennan, make sure he's being straight with us."

"So?"

"Here's what I found," he said, and he handed me the scrap of paper.

It was a small square sheet, almost completely covered by the black shading of a lead pencil, but in white letters plainly on the page some words stood out: PHIL-LIP TABER, ROOM 7, PORT CITY COURT.

TWELVE

The Port City Court, a single, long, brown-shingled motel, stared directly at the highway that crossed its line of vision. Parked cars had their noses all but pressed against the room doors, tails inches away from fast-moving traffic. Every stall was filled, due largely to the steady flow of salesmen and college kids. Across the street was the Sandy's where John and I'd dined that noon; down from it was a shopping mall, as well as gas stations, a U-Haul place, a Dodge dealership, and more chain restaurants—that same stretch of businesses that seems to trail out to every town's city limits, where a sign gives the population and says what that town's middle name is. In Port City it was prosperity. But what the sign didn't say was that prosperity's middle name was Norman.

Sitting behind the desk in the manager's office, reading a confession magazine, was a young woman with a big nose that minimized otherwise pleasant features, and with platinum hair that was worn in the same style (sprayed beehive) she'd used some half a dozen years before to trap her high school steady. Half a dozen years was also about how long it'd been since I'd seen this woman, her name long since escaping my memory.

"Oh," she said, raising dulled eyes which momentarily lighted up, "well, if it isn't . . ." And she touched her cheek and nodded quickly in pretense of remembering more than she did, not realizing she had just established for me that we had something in common.

"Long time no see," I said.

"Long time," she said. "Long time. Good to see you again, after so long."

"Good to see you."

"Say," she said, "whatever happened to, uh . . ." She touched her cheek again. "That girl you . . ."

I shrugged. "I don't know. Kind of lose track, you know. Did you and, uh, ever get married?"

"Yes," she said, "but we split up. I got the boy, though. Real cute kid. He's in the fourth grade this year."

"What's his name?"

"He was named after his father."

"Good. That's good."

"Ain't seen you since high school."

"I lived out of town for a while."

"Those was fun days."

"Yeah, they were fun, all right."

"You didn't want a room, did you?"

"No, no. I'm living here in town again. I've come to see a guest you have here. Friend of mine. Phillip Taber?"

She looked down her register, sliding her finger down the page as she did. "Yeah, here he is. Taber. Room seven. Checked in 'bout noon. I wasn't on duty then."

I smiled at her; suddenly I flashed on sitting across from her in a study hall. I said, "He called me this afternoon and said he was in town, staying out here. I'd sure like to surprise ol' Phil. Kind of . . . pop in on him, you know?"

"Oh sure. Well, hey, why don't you take his spare key here and do that?"

"Could I?"

"Boss might frown, but what the heck? Ain't as if I don't know you." She reached behind her on the wall of keys and plucked one off. "Here you go."

"Thanks."

"Sure," she said, returning to her magazine.

Just as I was going out the door, her voice behind me said, "Nice seeing you again, and talking."

"Yeah, nice talking to you, too."

There was music, hard loud rock music, behind the door to room seven. Tiny fingers of gentle smoke were crawling out around the door's edges, bearing the fragrance of burning incense. I put my ear to the door and heard no one speaking, but that didn't necessarily mean it was safe to assume Taber was alone. I looked around a couple times, catching sight of a shining new green Javelin in the stall adjacent to the room, and then went ahead and worked the key in the lock.

The lights were out, so as I went in I hit the switch.

He was on the bed, on his back, shirt off, wearing nothing but faded bell-bottom jeans. His chest was pale and hairless, but his face was fully bearded and the hair on his head, while showing signs of thinning, was frizzily long. A joint was tight in his lips, and he was caressing it easily with the fingers of one hand; he drew a long toke on it. On the nightstand next to the bed was the stick of burning incense, but even with that hanging in the air the pervasive smell of the joint's smoke couldn't hide. From past experience I made it as more than simple pot—more like hashish. Maybe it was some of that smack weed that was going around, pot cured in heroin.

He didn't react right away. He just stayed right on his back looking up at the ceiling, the only sound coming from him being the sucking in on the cigarette.

I shut the door and went over to a bureau opposite the bed where a cassette tape player's twin speakers were putting out the music. I turned it down.

All at once he came off the bed at me, like a threshing machine made out of skinny arms and legs and hair, and my back was to the wall and his bony fists were crashing again and again into my ribs. I pushed his head away with the heel of my hand and sent him down with ease, like I'd batted a weighted punching dummy, but he came back the same way, bounced right up and a sharp, hard little mallet of a fist jacked my eye, and then another jarred my stomach, and then my eye again, and the "V" point of an elbow shot pain through my balls and from there, in increasing waves, throughout my body, and suddenly I was on the floor and Janet Taber's common-law mate, a hideous scarecrow come to life, was raising a bare foot to stomp me, yelling, "Don't mess with my karma, man!"

Simultaneously I caught my senses and his foot, and I heaved him in the air. He thudded softly on the bed and I ran over and held him down on it with a straight-arm and said, "Easy man, I didn't mean to bring you down, come on man, let's cool it now."

I cooed at him like that for a while, and finally he settled down. He didn't *come* down—that smack weed or whatever the hell he was on was too potent for that—but I was happy to have him just floating in one spot.

"Phil Taber?"

He looked at the left corner of the room and concentrated on something—a mote of dust, maybe, or a piece of lint—and his smile flickered. I took that to mean yes.

"Janet was your wife?"

He nodded, and as he did, a convulsion took hold of him and made his whole body nod with him.

"What are you doing in Port City?"

His voice was soft, almost inaudible, but I heard him say: "Hey, man, I ain't *that* fuckin' high." And a cackle ripped out of him with the abruptness of an ambulance siren.

Damn. That was bad. He was a laugher—somebody for whom getting high was an intensification of life's absurdities. Which meant he would let out a peal of laughter at just about anything, everything.

"Listen," I said. "Listen to me. Are you so high you don't care whether or not you get busted? You best talk things over with me or I'll have the sheriff on your butt so fast you'll think you're hallucinating."

The cackle turned into a more or less normal laugh, which kept going as he said, "Call him . . . go ahead, ya stupid jerk, go ahead and *call* the Man."

That stopped me.

"You talked to him already?" I said.

His smile flickered yes.

"Gave him permission for the autopsy?"

His smile again said yes and he laughed some more.

I didn't know how much of this to buy, so I asked him, "What's the sheriff's name, since you know him so well?"

He then did a very bad impression of Walter Brennan that was just good enough to make his point.

I said, "Brennan knows you're a user?"

" 'Just be out of town by sunrise,' is all he says, 'Yessir, Mister Dillon,' I says."

"What about Janet? Doesn't it mean anything to you she's dead?"

He stopped cold for a moment, no laughter, no smile, but his eyes still fixed on some remote fleck of dust. He said, "Man, you and me we're dyin' right now. You're born and then you start dyin'. Big fuckin' deal."

"What about your son? Any feelings about him?"

He shifted his focus of attention to the right corner of the room. He smiled again, this time not at me. It was neither yes or no.

"What about your son?" I repeated.

"What son? I don't have a son . . . son . . . sunrise . . . out of town . . . 'Yessir, Mister Dillon,' I says. Get outa my karma, man."

I released my hold on him but he stayed put anyway. I got up and roamed restlessly around the room. I looked in his suitcase: one newly purchased, now-wrinkled dark dress suit; some soiled underwear; no heavy dope, other than a lid or so of that admittedly strong grass; a rental slip for the Javelin outside; and the last half of a round trip ticket in a Pan Am envelope. On the outside of the latter was his time of arrival: eleven that morning; he'd come in from Chicago. That pretty well ruled out any thoughts I might've had, after his spirited attack on me, about him being a possible suspect in the beating of Janet's mother and the burning of the house. The only other item in the suitcase was a recently bought shiny black leather billfold. The only identification in it was a crinkled-up, dirty driver's license—Illinois, expired—and there was some cash in it. Five crisp, new bills.

Five thousand dollars.

I rushed over and grabbed one of his skinny arms and said, "Where the hell did you get money like this?"

He grinned at the ceiling.

"Answer me!"

He kept grinning. "One of my paintings, man."

"Yeah, I heard you were an artist." I shook him. "What did you do for this kind of cash? Who'd you rip off?"

He said, "Turn on th' music."

A thought came to me from out of left field.

"Norman," I said.

Somewhere in the glazed, dilated eyes a small light seemed to go on.

I grabbed a thin arm. "Norman—what's that name mean to you? Norman? Norman!"

He started back in on a laughing jag and I got in the way of the stale warmth of his musky breath. Another whiff and I'd get a contact high. He said, "Turn on th' music. Get outa my karma."

I let go of him. Got out of his karma. Threw the billfold on the nightstand, by the stick of melting incense.

On my way out I turned his cassette player back up; the rock group Deep Purple was playing an instrumental called "Hard Road."

Taber and I liked the same music. For some reason that made me feel a little sick.

Or maybe I just wasn't used to the smell of pot smoke anymore.

PART THREE

NOVEMBER 28, 1974

THANKSGIVING

THIRTEEN

I knew where the Filet O'Soul Club was, but I'd never been inside. In my mind there still lingered, from impressionable high school days, the nasty stories that filtered down from the Quad Cities, stories that collectively formed the legend of the Filet O'Soul.

The club was in Moline (which is on the Illinois side of the Quad Cities), up on the Fifteenth Street hill where it starts to level out, just at the point where you can't see the cars coming up over, and crossing the street becomes a jaywalker's Russian Roulette. A lot of people drove top-speed through that little two block section, where the Filet O'Soul was just one of a cluster of small businesses that shared little in common outside of a general lack of respectability. Nice folks resented the fact that this accumulative eyesore was on a main drag like it was, but there wasn't much a person could do about it except roar up over the hill now and then and scare hell out of pedestrians.

But the Filet O'Soul, unlike some pedestrians, was anything but run-down. The outside was shiny black pseudo-marble—a smooth glassy dark front with no windows, with a big shiny steel door recessed in its center and a little neon sign above the door spelling out the club's name in red against black. The Filet O'Soul was said to be an extremely clean bar, with excellent food, beautiful, efficient waitresses, the best bartenders around, solid entertainment and reasonably low prices. The only dent in a reputation otherwise as solid as the club's steel door was its legend: nobody white who went in ever came out in one piece.

When I was in high school, every month or so John and I and a carload of guys would go up to see the skin flicks at the Roxy Theater, which was a couple doors down from the Filet O'Soul. I can remember the butterflies in my stomach as I'd walk past the place with my buddies, heading for the safety of the Roxy's hard seats and stale air, trying to ignore the milling blacks smoking out front of the Filet, hoping they wouldn't say anything, hoping they wouldn't kill us or worse, paying dearly for the sin of the Roxy.

Such was the feeling I had Thanksgiving morning when Jack Masters called to tell me he'd arranged a meeting for me with Rita Washington at the Filet O'Soul.

But after a second the feeling went away, and I hadn't, I hoped, let any of it show over the receiver to Jack. Great, I said to him, what had he told her?

Just that I was an okay guy, he said, and that all I wanted was talk. That I was a writer, but not a reporter—just a mystery writer researching something for a story. And, since she was a part-time school-teacher who could use the money, that there was twenty bucks in it for her.

I told him he was awful free with my money and he said *nothing's* free, son; then I asked him what time he'd set it for.

Eleven o'clock this morning, he told me, and nobody'd be there but the bartenders, getting ready for the crowd that'd be in to watch the football games on TV. Rita knew one of the bartenders pretty good and he'd given the okay, Jack said.

I thanked him for all the trouble, and he said, well, he wasn't going to let me go up there myself night before a holiday. Hadn't I heard what they said about the Filet O'Soul?

The door's steel was cold on my knuckles as I knocked. I stopped knocking and waited a few moments, was getting ready to knock again when the door opened. The man who answered was tall and lean and wore a black satin long-sleeved shirt with a red patent leather vest and black brushed corduroy pants. Skin coal black, nostrils wide, eyes dark and alert, forehead, cheekbones and chin chiseled, smile white, slow, careful and amused—he looked like a charcoal drawing, and a good one.

"You'd be Mallory," he said.

I nodded, smiled liberally.

"Rita isn't here yet," he said.

"Oh," I said.

"You want to come in and wait?"

"Please."

He opened the door and I stepped in. But would I ever step out again?

The room was a long rectangular box, lined with booths; the lights were up full, but the room was still pretty dim. About halfway down, a guy was sweeping dirt into a dustpan, his uniform identical to the bartender's, though faded, and matching the floor's red and black tiles, which were also faded. I watched as the bartender walked to the far left corner of the room to the semicircular bar, which he got back behind, and started polishing glasses. I went over to a booth and sat down. The guy swept his last pile of dirt into his dustpan, and as he carried the filled pan away, he cut the lights, with the only remaining illumination coming from small red bulbs under the abstract prints by each booth and a few lighted plastic booze ads at the bar and elsewhere. Immediately the place looked better, and was on its way to having "atmosphere": all that was lacking was smoke and people.

After I'd waited ten minutes, the bartender came over and put a glass of draw beer down in front of me.

"You looked dry," he smiled.

I thanked him and dug for some change in my coat pocket.

He just smiled and shook his head no, with an odd mixture of friendliness and condescension.

I thanked him again but he was already on his way back to polish glasses behind the bar.

When I was halfway through the beer, the door opened.

She was tall: five-nine at least; a slender young woman, almost thin—though nothing was missing—wearing a purple pantsuit with a turtleneck sweater peeking up over the collar, the sweater a deep purple, the suit a lighter purple. Her skin was the color of milk chocolate. Her face was wideset, with heavy-lashed big brown eyes; pouting, flower-petal lips; strong, angular cheekbones; and a gentle, almost delicate nose, the kind people go to plastic surgeons to get, though her nostrils had a hint of the proud flare that money can't buy. Her hair was up, Afro-style, but was straight, and a coal-black contrast to the light brown skin.

She came over and looked at me with the big-lashed eyes not blinking and said, "Mallory?"

I stood. "Yes, Miss Washington?"

"Rita," she said, and sat down while I was still in midair.

"Mal," I said, sitting back down.

"Mal," she said, neutrally, a verbal shrug.

I said, "Thanks for coming, Rita."

"You mind telling me something?"

"Not at all."

"Why am I here?"

"You don't want to be?"

"I'm half an hour late, aren't I?"

"Listen, if you're worried this is going to be some kind of come-on . . ."

"I wasn't worried about that—not till I came in here and you sat there looking at me with your mouth open."

I felt the red crawl up out of my neck. "I'm sorry, I didn't expect . . ."

"What *did* you expect?"

"Let's start with what I didn't expect, which is the best-looking woman I've seen in . . ."

"A coon's age?" she said. "Save it. This better start sounding like something besides pussy hustle, and quick."

"Hey, nothing like . . ."

"I should've known what the twenty

bucks was for." She started to get up. "Happy Thanksgiving, turkey. I'll see you."

"Wait. No hustle. Please wait."

She hesitated.

"Just listen to something and let me ask you a couple questions. Take the twenty just for listening." And I laid two tens on the table.

"Questions about what?"

"Why don't you listen first?"

"Why don't you tell me why I should?"

"It concerns a brother of yours."

"I got lots of brothers."

"Not that kind of brother."

"I got a lot of that kind, too. Six of them." She pushed the two tens on the plastic tabletop away. "None for sale."

"Is one of your six brothers missing an eye?"

"Why, did you find it? Screw off." She started up again.

"Wait. Please."

Again she hesitated, sat back down in the booth. She sat silently for a moment, then brushed the bills aside and said, "Why don't you just put the twenty away? It gives me a cheap feeling."

"It's not enough, you mean?"

"I mean nothing I got is for sale."

"Listen, I didn't mean to . . ."

"My brother likes privacy. If that's what he wants, that's okay with Rita, and there isn't a price on it."

"Will you do this much? Will you listen to what I have to say and then decide?"

She sighed.

I told it to her, but in a different order than I'd been using; I got out my violin and started with Janet's end of the story, the kid with heart trouble, the mother beaten and left to die in the burning house, the Colorado Hill "accident" that echoed Senator Norman's earlier fatal crash, with the part about the one-eyed guy who was maybe her brother in the middle of the story, ending with the encounter I'd had with Phil Taber last night.

"What about your friend's stepdaddy?" she said, interested in spite of herself. "If he's the sheriff, you ought to be able to get the straight shit on this Taber dude from him."

"No way," I said. "Brennan was out last night, and didn't answer the message I left for him with John, which was to call me whenever he got in. I went over this morning and he was off somewhere else. Besides, he isn't likely to cooperate with me, anyway."

While I'd been talking, a few black guys, ranging in age from twenty-one to thirty-five, had wandered in, taking seats at the bar and settling down to watch the football game on the color TV that sat perched above the mirror behind the counter. A few of them gave me wary looks, but nobody hassled me.

But then Rita asked me to go over and get something for her at the bar, and I went after it, and while I was getting it a thin, tall, bushy-haired black in an Afroprint shirt and gray bell-bottom slacks ambled over to the booth and started chatting with Rita.

I came back with Rita's drink in hand and caught what he was saying: "... messin' with the white meat again, Rita baby?"

Rita wasn't saying anything.

The guy went on. "Still teachin' in the white man's school, baby? Still wiping the white man's nose? Shit, girl, you make me wanna puke."

I said, "Excuse me."

He looked at me out of the corner of an eye and he sneered. He was still facing Rita, away from me, but I could tell who the sneer was for. "Who's the honky, baby? Got him talked into buyin' your bleach for you, and scrub you down?"

I said, "Suppose you just leave us alone, friend."

He turned and looked at me. "Don't give me that friend jive, mutha—"

I said, "Don't give me that mutha jive, friend."

I saw it coming and ducked, tossing the drink up into his face and bringing a knee up into his stomach as his arm sailed over me. I stepped out from under him and elbowed his back and he went down on his belly.

I leaned against the booth now, catching my breath, wondering why I hadn't started to shake yet. I watched him push up on his hands, get to his feet, and go into a crouch. He was smiling. Not that he'd warmed to me or anything.

I was outclassed, but what the hell. It wouldn't be the first time I had the crap kicked out of me. Just so I could hang onto my teeth.

But three guys had started over from the bar. They were black, of course, and two of them were very big: six feet-two, one of them was, and fat, and the other was a wiry six-four. The third was short but bulging with muscle.

Now I started to shake.

They came up slowly behind my crouching friend, flanking him. The tall wiry guy grabbed him by the shoulder and spun him around. He said, "You wanna leave these folks alone, or wear your butt for a hat?"

Before my friend could answer, the tall fat one grabbed his other shoulder and dragged him back to the bar.

I said, "Thanks," to the remaining two, and they shrugged noncommittally and headed back for the bar.

I turned to Rita who hadn't said a word through it all.

She said, "You spilled my drink."

I laughed and shook my head.

She looked at me with the big brown eyes; she blinked once, those lashes damn near fluttering, then said, "Let's get out of here."

"Oh?"

"Let's go to my place."

FOURTEEN

She pulled her white Mustang along the curb in front of Lange's Sporting Goods, and I edged the Rambler into the space directly behind hers. Though the sidewalks and streets of downtown Rock Island were all but deserted, Rita moved as though she were afraid of being seen: she got out of the Mustang and walked quickly to a doorway that separated the sports shop from its record store neighbor, and she opened the door, stepping inside, and held it open for me. All of this she'd done before I had the keys out of the dash.

I humored her by getting over there and inside with her as fast as possible, and followed her up old wooden steps that weren't too crazy about being walked on. Then I stood while she worked her key in the door, which had white paint flaking off

121

it like the hall around, and that door too she held open for me and we were inside.

The walls were purple. Deep purple like her sweater. That is, they were three-quarters purple, with the bottom quarter white. The rug was a rich, thick shag, also purple. Light, like her pantsuit.

The apartment was one medium-sized room, with no furniture proper, only things. Things like sizes and shapes and colors of pillows scattered about; a transparent inflatable chair; a homemade desk of cement blocks supporting a slab of dark wood, with typewriter and papers and books on it; a stool for the desk; a portable TV; component stereo with stack of albums; a bookcase, also homemade with cement blocks, running the length of and a third up the wall opposite the doorway. The adjacent wall was taken up by the door to the bathroom and to my immediate left as I stood in the entryway was what might be described as a kitchenette-ette: a single cabinet over a small refrigerator and smaller stove, obviously very old, huddling in the corner like two squat midgets. On the other side of the entryway, part of the wall jutted out a foot or so and had on it a rectangular outline which meant the pregnant wall was bearing a Murphy bed. On it were posters of Paul Newman and Malcolm X.

"Some odd couple," I said, a little wryly, nodding at the posters.

"Not really," she said, mildly defensive, sitting on the fluffy carpet and leaning catlike against a red pillow. "Paul Newman's very political, too."

I glanced around the purple room. "Who's your interior decorator? Welch's?"

She smiled. Her teeth were small and white, maybe a bit too small—thank God, an imperfection at last.

"Ghastly, isn't it?" she said, gesturing with a long-nailed hand. "Well, there's a reason for this purple pad, outside of that being a pet color of mine. It's hard to find decent apartments, you know? And the only teaching job I was able to land was part-time English instructor at a junior high because even though I have my four years of college, I didn't take enough education courses, and now I'm on temporary teaching certificate, and they're making me take some classes at Augustana College to pick up the hours I lack. That's why that twenty bucks of yours looked good to me, incidentally."

When she didn't go on, I said, "Just how does that explain your purple passion?"

"Oh. Well, anyway, I wanted something cheap in an apartment to tide me over till I could find and afford a nice place. So I ran across *this* place, and it was horrible—

all of it peeling paint like the halls out there—but it was cheap for downtown so I took it anyway and got permission from the landlord to have it de-bugged and repainted and carpeted. At my expense, of course, *but*, I figured if I made it look nice, in a conventional way, you know, painted it some standard pastel and wall-to-wall carpet, my bastard landlord'd up the rent on me. Ever had that done to you, Mallory? Where you put money into fixing up an apartment and then get your rent hiked on you for your trouble?"

I nodded. "The way this place is now," I said, "your landlord's probably afraid you'll move out and saddle him with this purple elephant."

She laughed gently and started unbuttoning the top part of her pantsuit. She slipped out of the coat and folded it in half and tossed it over on another big pillow. She straightened her sweater, pulling it down, and I did my best not to look at her breasts as she did, and I failed. She didn't seem to mind. She patted the pillow next to her and motioned for me to sit down and I did.

"So you're a mystery writer?"

"Trying to be. Selling a few short stories."

"That's really exciting. Where do you ..." She stopped, smiled. "I was about to ask you where you get your ideas. Listen, are you in a hurry? Got some big Thanksgiving spread to get back to Port City for?"

"No."

"That's where you're from, isn't it? Port City? Or do you just go to Jack Masters's school down there?"

"Both."

"So your family isn't having a big deal or anything?"

"My folks died a while back."

"Oh."

"And, unlike you, I'm an only child."

She ignored my graceless attempt to get back on the subject and stared at me with big unblinking brown eyes and said, "Thanksgiving isn't Thanksgiving without a turkey dinner."

"Let me write that down."

She threw a pillow at me.

"All right," she said. "So maybe I do sound childish, maybe it is a cliché, but man, that's how it is with me. If you'd had a big family, you'd know. Now *my* old man, no matter how tough things were, and they were plenty tough sometimes, he'd make sure there was a bird on the table Thanksgiving. Always."

"No family get-together today for you either, Rita?"

"Well, that much we got in common, Mallory. My folks are dead, too. I was the youngest of seven kids, and, well, we kind of drifted apart and we just never get together."

"How about you and your brother?"

"Listen, if you think I'm not aware of the direction in which you are trying to swing this conversation, you better check out of this hotel *now*. I'm *thinking* about talking to you about that, but I'm not sure yet. Let it work itself out, will you?"

"Rita."

"What?"

"How about I take you out for a turkey dinner? Surely there's a restaurant around here somewhere serving a Thanksgiving buffet or something. What do you say?"

"That's a sweet bribe, Mal, but . . ."

She called me Mal instead of Mallory. A good sign. "Hey, come on, Rita, what do you say? Had any better offers?"

"It's just that it isn't necessary, Mal. I can fix us turkey right here."

"Here?"

"Sure."

"That's a lot of trouble, isn't it? I mean, can you do that?"

She got up and said, "Stay put," and walked over to the kitchenette-ette. She bent down and opened up the little refrigerator. She took out two packages and held them up for me to see: Turkey TV dinners.

I grinned and nodded my approval.

A few minutes later, after she put the

dinners in the oven, she came back and lay down against the pillows, facing me.

"Why'd you ask me up here, Rita?"

She shrugged.

"You still think I'm trying to hustle you out of your clothes?"

"No," she said, "but you wouldn't mind it if it happened."

"*I* wouldn't. How 'bout you?"

"Don't know yet. Too early."

"You aren't hustling *me* now, are you, Rita? Just a little?"

"Oh *sure*. *I'm* hustling *you*."

"It's possible."

"I know. I'm hot just lookin' at you."

"Come on. How do I know you aren't covering for your brother? Maybe he's in trouble up to his butt, and you want to help him by getting me distracted. Maybe any minute now you're going to start pumping *me* for information."

"If that's what you think," she said, her voice a little cold now, "try laying one of those white paws on me and see what happens." She ran a long fingernail gently down my cheek.

"Rita, if we're neither one of us hustling each other, if we maybe kind of like each other a little, couldn't we just talk about your brother now and get it out of the way?"

"You know, I'm beginning to wish those

guys back at the Filet O'Soul wouldn't've helped you out."

"Look, this isn't a game with me. A young woman's dead and nobody cares."

"Nobody but you. The white knight."

"Damnit, are you going to help me or not, Rita?"

"Sure, Mallory, sure. I'll help *you* out, a total stranger. I'll dump on my brother for you, 'cause you seem like a nice guy and I like your looks and you tell a mean story."

"Rita."

"What?"

"Why'd you ask me up here?"

"I wish I knew," she said. And she turned away, the pouty look of her lips growing poutier. Then she slid around and brought her face up to me and pressed her mouth against mine.

The kiss lasted quite a while for a first kiss, but it was soft and tentative, not hot and bothered. Her lips were full and rich and sweet and the sensation was both gentle and heady.

When the kiss was over, I leaned forward to kiss her again, but she moved away and smiled. It wasn't a bitch smile, either, not a tease: she was saying, let's not rush this, let's take our time, *please*.

She let me take her in my arms and hold her, and we lay like that on the floor, resting against the pillows, Paul Newman and Malcolm X watching us, and we stayed that way, not saying a word, not even kissing again, until somewhere a sharp little bell rang and she bounced up.

"What the hell was that?" I said.

She was over by the stove. "Turkey time," she said.

A couple minutes later we were sitting like Indians, eating out of the aluminum TV dinner trays and sipping cold beers.

"You're a great little cook," I said.

"Aw shut up."

"No really, it's good."

"It's hot anyway."

"It's hot and it's good."

"It's turkey."

"It's Thanksgiving."

She smiled. "It's Thanksgiving."

We toasted beer cans.

We ate in silence for a few moments, then she said, "This, uh, thing 'bout the, uh, dead chick . . ."

"Yeah?"

"You were trying to tie in a guy named Norman?"

"Several guys named Norman. There's old man Norman—that's Simon Harrison Norman—and there's his son Richard—he's the dead one who was a senator—and there's Stefan Norman—he's the nephew who's running the Norman Fund, whatever that is. How's that for confusing?"

"My brother works for the Normans."

"What? What did you say?"

"My brother Harold works for the Normans. Harold has one eye and he's very big and for the last ten years or so he's worked for the Normans. In Port City."

"The hell you say."

"One of the guys he works for is this Stefan Norman. He lives across the river in Davenport. You want me to take you to see him?"

FIFTEEN

I pulled the Rambler into a place between a Lincoln Continental and a Grand
Prix, making mine the only car in the
whole Nottingham Acres parking lot without a vinyl top. Nottingham Acres was
a big fancy U-shaped Tudor building whose
grounds probably consisted of a mere acre
or less, but why get technical? Besides,
with the rent this joint probably charged,
how could they get away with calling it
Nottingham Acre?

"I'll wait here in the car," Rita said.

I said, "You'll what?"

"I'll wait here in the car."

"You'll wait here in the car."

"That's what I said."

"What happened to 'I'll take you to see
Stefan Norman'?"

"This is where he lives. Top floor of this wing facing us right here. Number 1207."

"You're something else. What is it, you afraid you'll get your brother in trouble if Norman sees you helping me?"

"That's part of it."

"What else is there?"

"You might do better without me. The other time I saw Norman I didn't get along too well with him."

"What was that about? He make a pass?"

"Hardly. It was about my brother's job."

"Well. I know better than to ask you anything about that."

"You're learning."

"Okay. You'll wait here in the car."

She nodded.

The outside of the building was made up of rough, varicolored blocks of stone, but inside everything was lush wood, like a table. There was a single elevator, self-service. It surprised me a little that there was no elevator attendant (nor for that matter, doorman or parking lot attendant), but that could be put down to Thanksgiving or technology or cutting corners. Like the acres Nottingham didn't have.

As the elevator opened on the twelfth floor, Norman's apartment was directly across. The door had 1207 on it in gold numbers, and was a big solid chunk of wood.

I knocked.

It took a while, but finally the door opened halfway and the opening was filled by a short, small-boned man in a long-sleeved light blue shirt with floppy pointed collars; the shirt was untucked and hanging down almost to thigh level on darker blue, also floppy bell-bottom trousers. His hair was black and curly and oily and long, his cheeks pockmarked and prominently boned, his nose hooked, and his eyes a light gray blue under thick brows. The eyes were intense, the kind of intense that holds you and can make you forget the rest of a slightly repulsive countenance.

He gave me a hesitant smile; his teeth were very good: too good.

"Have we met?" he asked. Hopefully, I thought.

"No, we haven't, and I hope you'll excuse this intrusion, Mister . . . Norman?"

"I'm Stefan Norman. Who are you?"

"My name's Mallory. I've got some urgent business I'd like to talk to you about. Could I possibly have a few minutes of your time?"

"Is this some sort of prank? Did somebody on ten send you up for some sort of prank?"

"No, no I assure you. Could I speak with you, please?"

An eyebrow arched. "That's exactly what you're doing now."

"Look, I know this is an imposition. . . ."

"Intrusion would be the word, Mr. Mallory, was it?"

"Yes, Mallory. It's very important. I drove up from Port City just to see you about it."

"Well, I see, Mr. Mallory. If you're willing to spend your Thanksgiving day afternoon on this project of yours, whatever it is, it must be important enough for me to spare you, I think you said, 'a few minutes of my time'?"

"I'd appreciate it, Mr. Norman."

"It does seem rather foolish, as I'll be available tomorrow morning, at nine, in my office in Port City. But, come in, come in."

He opened the door up the rest of the way, let me by, closed the door behind me, then moved in front of me and led me down a long narrow hall, long enough for the several doors on each side to open into good-sized rooms. The hall finally emptied out into a big, beam-ceilinged living room, bathed in coppery semilight from unseen fixtures up in the nonfunctional rafters. The two side walls of the room were paneled in rosewood with a conservative smattering of original abstract oils, but the room was dominated by the end wall, which was completely engulfed by a great stoneface of a fireplace, a moderate blaze befitting the time of year in its downturned mouth. Right of the mouth was a combination color television and stereo console in a heavy rosewood cabinet; on the tube was playing the final quarter of the football game the boys at the Filet O'Soul had been getting ready to watch not so long ago. The floor was rough slate, but three-quarters of it was covered by a rust-color shag carpet, and most of that was covered by a curving, overstuffed couch of plush brown leather facing the fireplace, with room enough in between for a mammoth black marble coffee table, which served as an auxiliary bar to its well-stocked, brown-leather-padded papa that covered most of the back wall. Between the bar/table and the couch were two rustic wooden stands that were, I supposed, the Nottingham version of TV trays; on them were plates of sumptuous if standard Thanksgiving fare of turkey-cranberries-mashed potatoes-etc. Somehow, though, I got the impression these boys felt they were roughing it.

I say "these boys" because Norman wasn't alone: he had a friend who was sitting on the couch, transfixed before the dancing images on the television screen. Norman cleared his throat and his friend rose from behind his tray and turned to greet us. He stood an inch or so over six foot and seemed sturdily built; his hands were big and roped with veins and hung loose on the ends of long arms. His hair was blond and very thin on top, with heavy, over-compensating brown sideburns; his forehead was broad over small, wide-set dark eyes and a tiny nose and tiny mouth. The weakness of some of his features was offset by a jutting, Steve Canyon-like jaw. He was wearing a yellow cashmere sweater and mustard bell-bottoms. He said, "Who's he?" His voice was equal parts sandpaper and sinus trouble.

Stefan Norman said, "His name is Mallory, he says. He came up from Port City to talk to me about something."

"What?"

"I don't know. Something, I said." He looked at me. "This is Mr. Davis."

"Hi," I said.

Davis nodded. "Funny time to drop in on people."

Norman said, "Go back and watch the game."

The big man shrugged, in a pouty way, and sat back down to his tray of turkey and reglued his eyes to the football game.

Norman said, "Would you like a drink, Mr. Mallory?"

"I didn't mean to interrupt your dinner."

"That's all right, I'd eaten all I cared to anyway. When you spend a lot of time preparing a meal, you become bored with the food even before you serve it."

I followed him over to the bar and sat down. Even the damn stools were covered with brown leather and stuffed like Chesterfield sofas. Norman said, "What would you like?"

"Anything."

"In the spirit of the great American sports fanatic, we've been drinking beer today. Well, malt liquor, really. How would that be?"

"Sure."

He got behind the bar and fiddled for a while, as though he had to brew the stuff himself, then handed me a filled glass. I drank half of it in two gulps, watching him as he stayed back of the bar, looking me over, trying to figure what to make of me, I guess. He sipped his glass of malt liquor.

I said, finally, "Did you know a girl named Janet Taber?"

He shook his head no. "No. No, I'm sorry."

"You might have known her as Janet Ferris."

"Ferris?"

"Yes."

"Ferris. No, but let me think. No, I don't think so."

"Think some more. She worked as a secretary for your cousin during his Senate campaign."

"She worked for Richard?"

"Janet Ferris."

"Janet Ferris. Hmmm. Now, wait, that wouldn't be that little girl from Drake? She was Richard's secretary, you say?"

"That's right."

"I do remember her, now. Attractive girl. Brunette, isn't she?"

"Well, she was a blonde when I saw her, but that's possible."

"You did say *was*, didn't you? And you did say *did* I know a girl named Janet Ferris? What does all this use of past tense mean?"

"She's dead."

"Oh. I'm sorry to hear that. She was such a nice, enthusiastic girl. A real help to Richard, if memory serves."

"She was killed in an automobile accident. Tuesday night. It was in the paper yesterday."

"I so seldom read the *Port City Journal*, living up here as I do."

"It was in the Davenport paper, too."

"At any rate, I didn't notice it. But I am sorry to hear it."

"The crash was on Colorado Hill."

"Really. I don't see yet, Mr. Mallory, how this concerns me."

"Richard Norman was killed in a crash on Colorado Hill."

"So have any number of people been, which is unfortunate, but what exactly has that to do with me?"

"Janet at one time worked for your cousin, agreed?"

"Agreed."

"She died in a crash on Colorado Hill. So did your cousin."

"And you see that as some kind of, what? Connective tissue? Linking thread?"

"You might say that."

"You're reading a lot into a simple coincidence."

"Coincidence, maybe. Not so simple."

He studied me for a moment. Then he said, "What exactly is your interest in all this, Mr. Mallory? Are you a detective, public or private?"

"I just knew Janet Taber, that's all."

"Then this is not a . . . an official investigation."

"If the cops were asking the right questions, I wouldn't have to."

He frowned; it was a thought-out frown. His facial expressions seemed calculated for the benefit of whoever he was talking to, rather than out of any real feeling or emotion.

"I hope," he said, "this conversation begins to gather significance soon, Mr. Mallory. Your 'urgent business' is proving to be the delusion of what appears to be a not terribly stable mind."

"You've come this far. . . ."

He sighed. "Continue."

"Do you know a man named Washington?"

"No."

"Are you sure?"

"Quite sure."

"He's a black man."

"How bothersome for him."

"He's big, and he has one eye."

"Is that right?"

"He's worked for your uncle for ten years."

"Has he?"

"He has."

Stefan looked at me, blankly.

I said, "And he has a sister named Rita."

"And how many eyes has she?"

"What are you up to, Norman?"

"I'm up to here with you, Mr. Mallory. I believe this conversation is over. Can you find the way out?"

"Thanks for the beer."

I trudged down the long hall and out the door and into the elevator and before two minutes were up I was again with Rita in the Rambler, and two people and one object were never more out of place as were we in the parking lot.

"Well?" she said.

I grunted. "He admitted knowing Janet, but only slightly. He claimed he didn't know she'd been killed in an accident. He also didn't respond to the name Taber."

"What do you make of that?"

"What do you make of this: he says he doesn't know you or your brother."

"You figure that adds up to something."

"It adds up to somebody's lying."

"Who do you believe?"

"You."

That surprised her. "Why me? Why not Norman?"

"First off, you're better looking."

"Gee, thanks."

"Second off, Norman isn't going back to Port City with me to arrange a meeting with a certain one-eyed gentleman. Right now."

SIXTEEN

Rita said, "I don't know how I let you talk me into this," and sat staring at the phone on the coffee table in front of her. The faces in the posters on my trailer walls seemed to stare with her.

I came over, bringing a cold bottle of Pabst and a glass and joined her on the couch. I filled the glass, pressed it into her hands. She sipped from it eagerly. I leaned back and took my time draining the bottle and several long minutes went by and I said, "Go ahead and call."

"I don't know."

"What don't you know?"

"This is such a shitty thing to do to my brother."

We'd gone back and forth about this all the way down from the Quad Cities, and though I still hadn't won her exactly, she

143

at least had agreed to come down with me and put the scene of the seesaw argument on my home ground. Her position was based on the premise that her brother Harold was incapable of committing and/or aiding-abetting a misdeed such as the one I'd outlined concerning Janet Taber. When I presented the bus station incident as counterevidence, she claimed that that *could* have been some other six-four, one-eyed black guy; besides, *her* six-four, one-eyed black brother wouldn't go 'round sporting a bare socket: he always wore an eyepatch.

I said, "This is not a shitty thing to do. It's a good thing to do."

"Shove it, Mallory, what does an only child know about it, anyway? And a white one at that."

"Prejudice rears her not-so-ugly head. Gimme back my beer."

"I drank it all."

I got up and went after another Pabst. When I came back she was leaning forward, her long-nailed fingers barely caressing the receiver. She caught me watching her, and jerked back. I filled her glass and sat back down beside her. I leaned back and drained the bottle and several long minutes went by and I said, "Go ahead and call."

"I been thinking."

"Great. Fine."

"You think Harold killed this Janet."

"I didn't say that."

"You said that this Janet ... what was her last name?"

"Taber."

"That this Janet Taber had her neck broken. That the accident was staged and somebody broke her neck."

"That's not the same thing as saying your brother killed her."

"You *implied* that my brother *could* do it."

"Well he probably could, if he was in the mood. One-handed. With or without eye-patch."

"You're such a son of a bitch, Mallory. Don't you know what this means, what you're asking?"

"Only you know that, Rita."

"Mallory. Mal."

"What?"

"I don't know. I just don't."

"Rita. Look at it this way. Suppose your brother *did* kill somebody. Wouldn't you say something should be done about it?"

"It would depend who he killed, and why."

"How about a woman. An unhappy young woman."

"Stop, you're making me cry. Tell me about the kid with heart trouble again, why don't you?"

"Okay, all right. No more hard sell."

"Why do you have to use *me?* Why can't you just go up to old man Norman's place yourself?"

"We went over that."

"Go over it again."

"Norman's property is fenced off. Private property, right? If your brother runs into me up there, a trespasser, after what I did to him the other day, there's not going to be enough left of me to put in a shoe box. Also, if what was left of me was turned over to Sheriff Brennan, he'd have a fine old time roasting whatever there was left to roast."

"I'm supposed to be a buffer between you and Harold."

"I was hoping you would be, yes. And you can get us officially past the gate up the hill."

"But when I call I'm not to tell Harold I'm bringing you."

"No. We'll surprise him and make his day. What do you say?"

"I don't know."

"Damn!"

"It's not an easy thing for me."

"Well, think it over some more, that's all I ask. You decide against it, I'll drive you back up to Rock Island whenever you say."

She looked at me, her eyes soft under the long lashes. She touched my cheek and

I started feeling like the manipulating bastard I was. I slid my arm in around her waist and kissed her neck and said, my lips against her ear, "Look, forget it, forget it. I'll do it some other way, or maybe I won't do it at all." And I meant it.

"But that's not right, either. . . . Mal?"

"Yeah?"

"Will you promise me something?"

"Sure."

"You'll keep an open mind—you won't prejudge anything."

I kissed her ear. "I'll go farther than that. No matter what it turns out your big black one-eyed brother did, I don't care if he eats babies and runs down old ladies, no matter what, I'll check with you and get permission before I make any move."

"If I say no cops?"

"Then no cops."

She slipped out of my arms and put her hand on the receiver again and said, "Thanks, Mal."

"Thank you, Rita."

She turned back to the phone under her fingertips and it rang and she jumped.

Then it rang again and she smiled and laughed nervously and I did, too. She picked up the receiver and handed it to me.

"Mal?"

It was John's voice.

I said, "How was Lori's turkey?"

"I'm in the middle of a slice of it right now," he said. "I sneaked in here to call you. I been checking off and on all afternoon, to see if you were back from the Cities yet. How'd it go?"

"Not bad. Wait'll you see what I brought back with me."

Rita elbowed me, but in a nice way.

John said, "Listen, I got to get back to the table before certain parties get wise. I know you were trying to corner Brennan last night and this morning—well, now's your chance. He's stuffing his face right now, and if you hurry over here you'll be able to catch him."

"Be right over." I slammed the receiver into the hook.

Rita's eyes said, "What?"

I said, "The town sheriff's finally available."

"You gonna go talk to him?"

"Yeah. You want to wait here for me?"

She nodded, eyes wide.

"This'll give you some time to think about that phone call."

"Okay, Mal."

"More beer in the fridge. But don't get bombed, I heard how you people get when you get bombed. Or is that Indians?"

"Mal."

"Yeah?"

"I'll have the call made by the time you get back. Either that or I'll be ready to go home."

I nodded. "Either way, kid," I said, and stroked her shoulder, got up, grabbed my jacket and headed out to the Rambler.

SEVENTEEN

Brennan choked on a bite of pumpkin pie when he saw me come in. He was the only one left sitting at the table eating; John and Lori's husband Frank were sitting on the floor in the far left-hand corner of the room watching yet another football game. John looked up as I entered and started to rise, but I motioned at him to stay put. Lori pulled out one of the empty chairs at the table and told me to sit. I did, and she brought me a big slice of pie with a heap of whipped cream on it.

"Hey, this is unnecessary," I said.

"You better eat it before Brennan does," she said. "He's on his third piece."

"I all of a sudden lost my appetite," Brennan said, and got up and went out into the kitchen.

I sat and ate my pie. I didn't hurry. John

came over and I told him about Rita and also about Stefan Norman. Then I thanked Lori for the pie and got up and went after Brennan.

He was sitting at the kitchen table smoking. He was wearing a blue sport shirt and tan slacks and seemed insecure out of uniform.

I sat down by him. "Got something against me, Brennan? I get this weird feeling you been trying to duck me."

"I got a lot against you," he said, sucking nervously on his cigarette, "not the least of which is you're a goddamn pain in the ass."

"I been trying since last night to see you."

"I didn't know that, or I'd come running."

"You going to tell me about Phil Taber, or do we play games?"

"You're the one playing games, Mallory. You're the mystery story writer playing private eye. And you're going to get your butt burned doing it."

"What's that supposed to mean?"

"Jesus Christ, Mallory. It's Thanksgiving, for God's sake. Can't a man have some peace Thanksgiving, spend a little time with his relatives and have some peace?"

"*Some* people get peace imposed on them."

"They die, you mean. Yeah, that happens to people."

"Sometimes they get killed."

"And sometimes they're in accidents. See? You're playing games again, Mallory, it's you who's playing games."

"Tell me about Phil Taber."

"What about him? He came to town because his wife was dead. He left. What about him?"

"You told John no immediate member of the family was available to okay the autopsy, that you got the court's permission to do it. Obviously it was Taber's permission you got, not the court's."

Brennan shrugged.

"Why'd you lie to John about it?"

"Because he'd tell you about it. Because he'd tell you about it and you'd go running after this poor guy and hound him in his . . . his, you know, hour of grief."

"Hour of grief, hell. I'd find out he was a doper, you mean."

"That wasn't it at all."

"Why didn't you bust him? You aren't exactly known for being soft on dopers around here."

"I won't claim I didn't realize he was a user, but he was from out of town, and doing us a favor, and it was a delicate time for him and he was told if he'd stay clean while he was in town and leave by the next morning, there wouldn't be no trouble."

Lori came in from the living room, clearing dishes off the table in there, and started stacking them up by the sink. Brennan gave me eye signals to keep my voice down.

I said, "What about Janet Taber's mother? Mrs. Ferris. And don't say, 'What about her?'"

"She was buried yesterday. So was her daughter."

"Buried?"

"The girl's husband paid to have them buried out at Greenwood Cemetery. Didn't have funerals for them, but I understand he laid out quite a sum for having some real nice stones put up for them."

"Nice stones. Phil Taber arranged all that?"

"He had a lot of money, and he was wearing a nice suit, and he seemed pretty straight, outside of that long hair and the pot smell on him. The nice suit didn't fool me, though. I knew what he was. He needed a bath."

"Are you looking into the mother's death?"

"What do you mean?"

"What I mean is Mrs. Ferris was beaten half to death before she was burned up in that house."

"That was the girl's story. Told to you. That makes it hearsay by the time it's reached my ears."

"Don't screw around with me, Brennan.

A doctor up at the University Hospital told that to Janet. Check up there and you'll find out."

"Why should I? I don't go nosing for trouble like some people I know. It comes my way, fine, I take care of it, otherwise I leave well enough. Believe you me, I got plenty on my hands just taking care of what comes my way."

"My God. What about the house? It *was* arson, wasn't it?"

"That ain't the way the fire chief sees it. Chief Nelson and his people looked into it yesterday morning and traced it down to some old papers and rags and cans of old paint out on the back porch. The building was a firetrap, too, one of them old wooden jobs, must've been near fifty, hundred years old."

"Brennan."

"What?"

"Are you covering up for somebody?"

Brennan bit down on his cigarette and gave me that practiced slow look of his and said, "I'm gonna pretend like you didn't say that."

"Then I'll have to say it again: are you covering up?"

"Before I break you in half, Mallory, how about you tell me just who I'd be covering up for?"

"Simon Norman, maybe. Stefan Norman? Both of 'em?"

"Come off it."

"You come off it. It's no secret the Normans controlled local politics for a long time, at least while Richard Norman was alive. Maybe they still do. Norman money, anyway."

"Don't you believe them fairy tales. You probably run across that shaggy dog about how old man Norman's supposed to be back of all the businesses in town. That's bull, all of it, bull."

"I saw Phil Taber last night."

"Good for you."

"He had five thousand dollars in his billfold."

"He did?" Brennan sat up, tried to cover his show of surprise by getting rid of his old cigarette and replacing it with a fresh one. "So what?"

"Where would Phil Taber get five thousand dollars?"

"How should I know? I don't know anything about him. Yesterday was the first and last time I ever seen him and that was for about ten minutes."

"The Normans could afford something like that, if they were buying him off. What would five thousand be to them? What did Phil Taber tell you in that ten minutes you spent with him? Outside of giving permission for the autopsy."

"Nothing."

"I don't believe you."

"Who cares? Since when are you the cop?"

"Just trying to live up to your sterling example, Brennan."

"All right, all right, he told me his wife and her mother didn't get along. That his wife was kind of crazy, she was one of them split personality types, you know? She was all the time beating up on her kid, and on the mother, too."

"And that's why you're not pursuing the angle about the mother being beaten up?"

"That's as good a reason as any. You want a solution to the big mystery, don't you? You feel you got to know the truth or you just can't go on? Try this one out: the little Taber bitch beats her mother up, and then goes out to spend some time with a friend, and while she's gone a fire starts up accidentally, so when she comes back the house is burning and her mother's dying, trapped in there and beat up; the girl gets feeling low over what she done, and boozes it up and goes off the cliff."

"No alcohol in the bloodstream, Brennan, remember?"

"Okay, so she was gonna go out drinking and had the bottle in the car with her. Still indicates the state of mind she was in, right? She was depressed and maybe a little suicidal and she drove off the cliff."

"And that's the way you see it?"

"No. I don't see it no way. I see some dead people, some accident victims, nothing more, nothing less. No foul play apparent. No arson, either. Principal player dead. The end. Case closed."

"You're through investigating, then?"

"I never started."

"She had a kid."

"Who had a kid?"

"I told you about it before. Janet Taber had a kid. You just said she used to beat her kid, remember? He's supposed to be in a clinic in the east waiting heart surgery. What about him?"

"He is his father's concern."

"Phil Taber, you mean."

"That's right. No worse off than a million other kids these days who gotta grow up with freaks for fathers."

Lori came over from the sink, where she'd been rinsing off dishes, and said, "Mal? Can I talk to you for a moment?"

"Sure." I looked at Brennan. "Excuse me, Sheriff."

He puffed at his cigarette, said nothing.

Lori took me into the nursery, which was a small room about the size of a double closet, with blue plaster walls. The lights were off. Her little boy Jeff was sleeping in his crib, so she talked in whispers.

"Excuse me for eavesdropping," she said,

"but I heard what Brennan said about Janet. What he said Phil Taber said about Janet."

"Oh?"

"Yes. Look I was talking on the phone this morning, with Annie Coe, about Janet. . . ."

"Who's Annie Coe?"

"Annie Coe's a girl about my age Janet was hanging around with these months since she moved back to town. She's divorced and she and Janet had a lot in common. Anyway, she's the friend Janet was with that night, the night of the fire and everything."

"And?"

"I don't need Annie's word for it to tell you that story about Janet being a split personality is a crock. I knew Janet well enough to peg that one as phony. And what Annie told me backs up my opinion. Annie said Janet and her mother had grown very close these past months. Janet felt her mother had really come through in time of need, you know? And though I never met Mrs. Ferris, Janet's mother, I know from what Annie said this morning that it's very unlikely Janet could have beaten up on her."

"Why's that, Lori?"

"You were with Janet, you know what she looked like. She wasn't big. She was almost petite. It must've been her father she took after, from what Annie said. What Annie said was, probably the only reason the beating and the fire didn't kill Mrs. Ferris right away was her size. Only reason she lasted most the night was that she was a big, healthy, fleshy woman. Stood close to six-foot. It'd take somebody good size to beat up *that* lady. . . ."

EIGHTEEN

There was a moon tonight, or a slice of it, anyway, but it was up under some clouds that were rolling by like dark smoke. Despite the darkness, I could see the Norman house plainly. The grounds directly surrounding it were free of trees and brush and sloped gently, very gently up around the house, which was outlined stark against the sky, sitting back from the edge of a hill that fell sharply to the Mississippi. The river's waters reflected what light there was back up against the smooth, unpainted cement walls of the Norman house.

It looked like a Moorish fortress or castle, as cut to scale and modified by a would-be Frank Lloyd Wright; something like some of the things put up in the thirties in California towns, only more so, and minus the stucco. The top floor sat on the bottom like a smaller box on a slightly larger one, with a one-story wing on either side; the roof was tower-cut, with fat, stubby turrets on every corner. In its original conception it had been a combination penthouse above and radio station below— the back wall still had the shadow where a giant radio antenna once climbed. The front wall, the face of the house standing watch over the river, had three irregular windows along the bottom floor, like odd teeth, and, on the upper floor, running near the house's width, a long horizontal window looking out on the river like the viewscreen on a welder's mask.

We had found the gate open, Rita and I, and had followed the narrow drive up to the house. The drive was bordered by thick dead brush and the occasional outstretching arms of a skeletal tree, all part of a thicket that served to isolate the Norman house and its sloping grounds, making it an island in the midst of a heavily populated section. That island was a part of the uneasy transition between downtown Port City and East Hill, with supermarket, filling station, hardware store and lumberyard just across the way, and on either side of the protective thicket were clusters of middle-class housing. The way to the gate of the Norman drive was via an alley bordered on either side by frame houses.

I got out of the car just before we cleared the thicket and turned the wheel over to Rita, let her drive up toward the house alone. I stayed back in the brush and watched her pull my Rambler into the open graveled area and park by the back door. There were no other cars in the parking area; opposite the house, across the graveled space, was an unpainted cement garage, built years ago for three cars, big enough now for two, at a slant.

About the time Rita would have been taking her keys out of the ignition, the back door to the house opened, and in the light it let out I saw a big black man come out and rush over to help her out of the car. He was wearing a well-tailored, well-cut houndstooth suit, with a white shirt, open at the collar, and he wore a black eyepatch where a left eye had been.

Harold Washington.

We'd met before.

He and Rita embraced, and with an arm around each other's waist, they went inside.

I approached the house carefully, staying within the confines of the thicket, and moved slowly around until I reached the point where the brush met the slope of the hill that dropped to the river. I crouched and stared at the building for something like five minutes, then crawled up by a slant-roofed wing, edged around it and went in through the same door as Rita and her brother.

I'd managed to get the layout of the house from Rita, so I wasn't worried about finding my way around. The door to her brother's living quarters was to my right and tight-shut, though soft sounds of conversation were seeping out. The game plan I'd outlined to Rita was that she would talk to Harold for half an hour, brother-sister small talk, and then break it to him she'd brought somebody along to see him. I had something else in mind, though, which necessitated a mild double cross.

The lobby I was in was boxlike, and its ceiling went the building's full two stories. The walls were smooth plaster, cream-colored, bare. A coatrack by the door was the only furniture, a tiny throw rug the only carpeting. The floors were well-varnished wood that yellowly reflected an overhead light. In the middle of the facing wall was an archway that cut through an otherwise enclosed hall.

I went over and stood within the hall. Its ceiling was as high as the lobby's. I checked my bearings: beyond the archway was the living room—big, sparsely furnished, much like an extension of the lobby, with various large, oddly shaped, undraped windows. To my right was a steep incline of stairs, no rail, crowded by claustrophobically tight walls.

I climbed the stairway, palms scraping against the confining walls, and at the top of the stairs found a landing. On the left was a door. I turned the knob and found the door unlocked and pushed it gently open and stepped in.

The room encompassed the whole top floor. There was no carpeting, again only bare, but well-varnished wood. The walls, too, were bare, except in the middle on the left where an artificial fireplace with elaborate woodworking stood dark and absurdly out of place in this cream-walled context. An oil painting of a pontifically smiling, handsome man in a purple suit and tie hung over the mantel, and on the mantel in front of the Rockwell-style portrait was a single silver-framed photograph. Along the end wall, with its long window looking over the Mississippi, the floor was raised half a foot, like a stage, and center-stage was a battered desk, coming up to the sill. The back wall was relatively crowded: a door in either corner—one I'd just come in, the other to a bathroom, I presumed—and a bed. Its head was to the wall, with a cluttered nightstand on one side and a dresser on the other, a wheelchair in front of the dresser, and a portable television on a movable stand in front of that. The bed had a man in it.

The man said, "Well. Hello. I don't believe we've met."

He was old. The bedcovers were tucked up under his arms, which lay straight and limp in front of him like the limbs of a ventriloquist's dummy. He was so old he was shrinking; the gray silk pajama top was sizes too big, a parachute he was lost in. The flesh of his hands was like parchment, and you could've stored things in the hollows of his cheeks. His hair was white and long, longer than mine, as though he didn't bother having it cut anymore. Though the handsome cast of his features hadn't been completely dimmed by time, the gray-blue eyes, once hypnotic and piercing, were milky and confused now.

"Hello, Mr. Norman," I said.

"Do . . . should I know you, young man?" The voice was resonant and not as old as the rest of him. "That is, I don't remember meeting you, but as you might guess, my mind is not all it once was."

There was a chair by the nightstand. I pulled it around by the bed and sat down. "We haven't met, sir," I said. "Excuse me for barging in, but I needed to see you."

He smiled, and in it you could imagine the masterful con man's smile it had been; unlike his nephew Stefan, Simon Norman's teeth were his own.

"I haven't received many guests in the past few years," he said. "But now, this particular moment, even an uninvited guest is welcome. It's Thanksgiving evening, you know, and the kind of time best not spent alone. If one can't share such times with relatives or friends, then a stranger will do. What was your name?"

"Mallory," I said, and offered my hand.

He took it. His grip was firm, but the flesh around it seemed ready to jump ship. The eyes got a little brighter and he said, "You aren't here to do me in, are you, Mallory? I didn't swindle your mother, did I? Or would that be grandmother? Did I swindle your grandmother out of her hard-earned dollars and are you here for retribution for that misconduct?"

"No," I said, "nothing like that."

"I must confess, if you were on, well, a mission of vengeance, you'd've picked a good night for it. You'd have a willing victim, as I've been rather melancholy this evening."

I nodded. "I understand."

"No, you don't," he said, sitting up somewhat straighter in the bed. "You assume I mean *guilt*, don't you? Well that's not it, not at all. Oh, hell, it was wrong of me, wrong to charge so high when times were so tough back in my clinic days. I was wrong. I *was* wrong, I'm first to admit it. Can you deny that? Hmmm?"

"I guess not."

"You know, I wasn't the black villain you'd think I was, if you heard those politicians tell it. The way they talked, bringing Richard down with all of it, and distorting it besides . . . hell. I gave them a lot of comfort, do you know that? Many people had hope, thanks to me. In their final days, even their final hours, they had hope because of me. False hope, you might argue, but it was hope, whatever kind, and real enough to them." He coughed. "You . . . you just try to put a price tag on that, try to say you can charge too much." He coughed some more.

I grabbed a stack of tissues off the cluttered nightstand and handed it to him. He coughed into one, crumpled it and tossed it on the stand.

He said, "People thanked me, you know."

I nodded.

"You don't know, you weren't born. Listen here, you see that desk back there? Back by the windows."

I nodded.

"Go over there and look at the top of it. Go ahead!"

I got up and walked across the room and stepped up on the platform by the window and looked down at the desktop. Under glass were photographs, aging, of varieties of people in snapshot poses, all of them with personal notes written on them thanking Simon Norman. In the middle was a signed photo of Herbert Hoover: "Best wishes, Doc Sy!" All of the inscriptions but Hoover's were in the same hand.

I walked back and sat down.

"What do you think of that?" he said.

"Impressive."

"Are you surprised?"

"Yes, I am. You seem in better spirits now."

He smiled and reached out and patted my shoulder. "I like having someone your age to talk to. You know, when you spend a holiday evening alone like this, it makes you reflective, makes you think on things—and people—that you've lost. My son, I lost my son, you know, did you know that? He might've been president one day. Before that May Belle, and now . . ."

"Now?"

"Say, did you look at the picture on the mantel?"

"No, I didn't."

"Go on over and look at it."

I got up again and went to the fireplace and lifted off the silver-framed photo. The portrait in purple smiled down at me as I looked at the photo, a studio shot of a pretty young woman, in the thirties manner: plump face, wide bright eyes, rosebud mouth, dark tight curls.

"Your wife, Mr. Norman?"

"She was a dancer," he said. His voice was soft now, as if in another room. "You never saw her feet touch the floor, that's how she danced. I took some patients down to Miami that winter and she was dancing in a club. Not just the chorus line, mind you, she was featured. Everyone loved her, but it was me she came back with and married. Ah, you should have seen this place then. White fluffy carpet, all the latest furniture, mirrors everywhere. She liked mirrors. Over there was where the baby grand was, a white baby grand; I hired a fella to come in and play on it now and then so she could dance. Over against the wall there was the bar, and oh, it was stocked with everything, you wouldn't believe . . . the funny thing is, she died of cancer, did you know that? Do you have any idea what it's like to help others and not be able to help somebody you love?"

"Mr. Norman."

"Yes, uh . . . Mallory, is it?"

"That's right. Mr. Norman, a young woman named Janet Taber died the other day. Did you know that?"

His eyes became cloudy again, then immediately hardened. "Yes," he said, "yes, of course, I mentioned that, didn't I?"

"No, you didn't . . . I . . ."

"Mallory. Mallory. You're the one Stefan called about. He said I shouldn't . . ." And he leaned over to the nightstand and pressed a white button.

I didn't bother moving. Five seconds later the door opened behind me and I didn't have to turn around to know there was a big black man back there waiting for me.

NINETEEN

Harold Washington said, "I'll make you a proposition."

I was sitting on a couch next to Rita in her brother's one-room living quarters on the lower floor of the Norman house. Rita didn't seem angry with me, though she wasn't pleased, either; apparently she felt my little whitey lie classified me more like kid-in-the-cookie-jar than Judas. I'd expected my confrontation with brother Harold to be rather on the short side; he'd show up and it would all be over but the shouting. Well, it wasn't over and there wasn't any shouting. He had quietly escorted me out of Simon Norman's presence, down the stairs and into his room, where Rita was waiting. And now Harold Washington was politely asking me if he could make a proposition.

I shrugged. "Propose away."

He said, "I have to go back up and give Mr. Norman his medication. If you'll wait here while I do that, I'll come back and answer some questions. Providing, of course, that you're first willing to answer a few of mine."

I managed to nod. Where was the cyclops-like, bus station brute of Tuesday past? Punjab, is that you, Punjab?

"Would you like me to bring you a cup of coffee when I return?"

I managed a second nod. What'd I do, knock human kindness into his head with that Pepsi bottle the other day?

"How do you like it?"

"Uh, black."

"Rita?" he asked.

"Nothing, thanks," she said. She seemed embarrassed, as if her brother's kindness and instant unspoken forgiveness was far worse than a scolding.

"Okay," he said, and he ambled out like a big tame bear.

I looked around the room, which was the reverse of the rest of the all-but-unfurnished house. The floor was carpeted in rich, wall-to-wall brown, and there was a large deep gold reclining chair next to the couch Rita and I were sitting on, with a coffee table between. From where I sat, the door was on my left and the wall surrounding it was the only one with its cream color nakedly showing. The wall behind me was paneled, and the wall across from me was a network of wooden shelves that housed not only a considerable library, but a component stereo, its various speakers, photographs of Rita and (I assumed) other Washington family members, a small but well-shaped ebony statue of a jungle cat and a hunk of driftwood; two-thirds down the wall the shelves gave way to closed cabinets, with a space in the center making room for a big color television. A single bed ran along the brown-draped back wall, next to an arched doorless closet in the corner.

"Your brother keeps a neat house," I said.

"Are you trying to make up?" Rita asked.

"No."

A few moments of silence limped by.

She said, "Why aren't you?"

"Why aren't I what? Trying to make up? Because you aren't mad at me."

"I'm not?"

"Hell, no. You know it wouldn't do any good."

"That I'll admit."

"And you know my motives are altruistic."

"You never stop bullshitting, do you?"

"I never noticed I was."

"You're right."

"I'm right about what?"

"My brother does keep a neat house."

"He sure does."

Washington came in, shutting the door with his foot as he balanced two cups of coffee in his hands. He came over to me and handed me a cup, set the other down on the table by the couch, then went over and pulled a chair off the wall and dragged it over by me and sat down. He was still wearing the houndstooth suit, and not even the absence of a tie made him seem any less formal. His bald head and lack of eyebrows seemed somehow less frightening than they had two days ago, and made him seem almost peaceful, monklike. The only tangible difference in his appearance from the other time we'd met was the eyepatch, which was large enough to hide the lengthy scar as well as the empty socket. But this difference was a major one: the raving madman seemed now a quiet and sane gentleman. Yes, gentle, damn it, which was, after all, what everybody'd been telling me about him.

"Mr. Norman asked me," he said, "to convey an apology to you for his abrupt show of bad manners. He said he enjoyed speaking with you, and hopes you aren't offended."

"Hardly. I was intruding."

"That," he said, sipping his coffee like a lady at a tea, "would seem as good a place as any to begin."

I wasn't fooled by any of this: I knew full well any moment he'd start pulling the arms and legs off me.

Rita said, "He was supposed to wait in the car, Harold, I was going to tell you ..."

"That's beside the point," he told her. "And I'm not at all interested in how he got you talked into smuggling him in here. I'm sure it took some nice footwork, but whatever it took, done is done, you brought him here and here he is." He turned back to me. "Now, do you mind telling me why you're sticking your nose in around here?"

I said I didn't mind at all. I told him how two days ago I'd seen him giving Janet Taber a very rough time in a bus station. I told him how that same night I saw her dead inside a car at the bottom of Colorado Hill. That she was supposed to be drunk-driving, only she didn't drink, and she was supposed to have died in the crash, but her neck was broken like maybe a couple big hands did it. That that was when I started sticking in my nose, and I found out she used to work for a guy named Richard Norman. Who also died in a car crash out at Colorado Hill. Son of that guy upstairs in the bed. Who a certain Harold Washington worked for.

"Have you noticed yet," I said, "that there're a few connections between these people and the incidents?"

"I see the connections," Washington said. "I just don't see yours."

"My connection is I liked Janet Taber."

"Knew her well, did you?"

"No. Somebody denied me that chance."

"And coming around here bothering Simon Norman is supposed to lead you to the somebody who did that."

"Maybe. The thought has crossed my mind that I'm talking to that very somebody right now."

Rita shifted nervously next to me.

"Mr. Mallory . . ." Washington began.

"Call me Mal. Do you prefer Harold or Harry? I hear some of your pals call you Eyewash."

"You've got balls, I'll give you that much. Brains, that I'm not so sure about. Do you really think I broke Janet Taber's neck?"

"You tell me."

"I didn't. Now ask me if I think it was a bad thing, her getting killed. Because I'll tell you it was a good thing."

"People getting killed is rarely a good thing."

He had something prepared for me, I could see it in his eye, something gone over in his mind he was now going to get to let loose.

He said, "This woman, this woman you knew for minutes, this woman whose posthumous honor you're out to protect, was a

back-stabbing, self-serving, blackmailing
bitch, and you better know that, know it
well, before you waste any more time on
her."

Rita said, "Hey, come on, brother, this
dead chick was all of *that*? You're laying it
on a little *heavy*, aren't you?"

"The only way you'd believe me," he
said to both of us, "is if I told you, in
detail, just what she was trying to put over
on Mr. Norman. And obviously, since I
wanted to see her kept quiet, I'm not
about to pass on to you the things that
died with her."

Rita said, her voice quiet, hurt, "You got
motive written all over you, Harold. No
wonder Mal thinks you might've done it."

I said, "He knows I've got him ruled out,
Rita."

Washington smiled and Rita said, "Oh?"

"Sure," I said. "If he was going to kill
Janet Taber, he wouldn't have gone into
that tough guy routine at the bus station.
He wanted to scare her off, not kill her off.
When that didn't work, it was too late to
kill her, if he'd wanted to, after the public
scene he'd just pulled."

"Balls *and* brains," Washington said.
"You're right. I took off my eyepatch and
went down there hoping to rattle her,
scare her off. I didn't know there'd be a
white knight around."

That's what his sister called me earlier.

I pointed a finger at the ceiling. "All of that just to protect that old man from something?"

He nodded. "That was the reason, and you're right again, he *is* an old man, a sad, sick old man. Who's paid and *re*paid and then paid some more for whatever wrongs he might've done."

"You can defend him. You're paid to."

"Come off it, Mallory. You saw him. Talked to him. Did you find him malicious? A ghoul? Did you want to strangle him with your bare hands?"

"Of course not."

He leaned forward in the chair and shook a thick finger at me. "He's been good to me. I've been with him ten years, and he's helped me help myself, help my family. How do you think Rita got her education? Ask her about the two brothers of ours that are in college right now, and on whose money. How do you think I came from ghetto and gang-fights to those books over on the wall? I wasn't even able to speak proper English before I came to him. He did it for me."

"What about those other people, years ago? Ones he didn't help?"

"Look, I happen to know that he personally has reimbursed as many families as he's been able to locate. His records were destroyed while he was in prison back in the forties, but by searching his memory and from people who contacted him, he was able to pay back much of what he took."

"And did he pay them interest? Did he give them a share of what he made investing *their* money?"

"I don't know why I'm even bothering with you, Mallory. You're just like everybody else, you probably don't even realize that a good deal of the earnings from Mr. Norman's various business holdings are turned over to cancer research—cancer and other diseases."

"A function of the Norman Fund, I assume?"

"Yes, but none of this has any relevance to your dead Janet Taber."

"Did the Fund give a research grant to Phil Taber?"

"Who?"

"My dead Janet Taber's husband. Perhaps it was a grant for research into the drug problem, since he's a doper himself. I saw him yesterday. Somebody rushed him into Port City, paid him at least five thousand dollars, and I suppose rushed him back out by now."

"What? What the hell are you talking about?"

"Now *you're* starting the I-don't-know-what-you're-talking-about-routine. Stefan Norman pulled it on me this afternoon."

"What?"

"He denied knowing anything about Janet Taber, except that a long time ago she worked for Richard Norman. And he'd never heard of Phil Taber, either, and you know what else? He denied knowing you. Why would he do that?"

Washington got up from his chair and said, "Probably because he's smarter than I am. He had the good sense not to encourage you. And I think I will, if it's not already too late, learn from Stefan's example, and ask you to leave. And take my sister with you, will you?"

TWENTY

I sneaked into my bedroom and reached across Rita, who was sleeping on her stomach in my bed, and groped around on the nightstand for a roll of Lifesavers. I brushed against her on the return trip and she shifted over on her back and let out a sexy little grunt and looked up at me, a bit shyly, pulled the sheet up to mostly cover her breasts and said, ". . . uh . . . haven't you been to sleep yet?"

Though the room was dark, my eyes were accustomed to it after an hour of insomnia and I could make her out very well. Her cocoa skin looked satin smooth, like skin in a retouched photo.

"Didn't mean to wake you," I said. A little embarrassed to be intruding on her privacy; and, as I was in nothing but my shorts, a little embarrassed, period.

"S'okay," she shrugged, sleepily.

"You want one?" I said, offering her a Lifesaver. "They're lime."

"N'thanks," she said, smiling crookedly. "G'night." She rolled back over on her stomach, and the sheet slid down and left her back bare; she was already asleep again.

I wanted to stroke her back. Bend over and kiss the small of it, run my hand over the rise of her buttocks. But I didn't. Instead I lifted the sheet up to her shoulders, tucked it around them, kissed her neck and whispered, "Goodnight," but she didn't hear me. I think.

I wandered back out into the living room and plopped back down on the couch, where I was spending the night, leaned my head back against the armrest and sucked on my Lifesaver.

Half an hour before, I'd given up on going to sleep: my mind was back trying to sort things out again. I'd managed to put all of it out of my mind, for a while, when after supper Rita and I had gotten into some friendly small talk—and some wine, which is why Rita was sleeping here tonight, since I didn't want to drive her back to the Cities tipsy. I think maybe both of us would've liked more than that to have happened, but we didn't let it—or hadn't so far; but with her sleeping nude in the next room, it was, shall we say, hard to sleep. Even without the rest of it to mull over.

After we left her brother at the Norman house, we'd stopped at the all-night supermarket across from the place and came back to the trailer and had a good time getting a late supper for ourselves. Rita made up a whole skillet of American fries while I broiled steaks and tossed a salad. There seemed to be an unspoken agreement between us not to delve further into the Janet Taber mess any more that night.

While we were eating, however, Rita began to tell me things about her brother, in an offhand casual way, and though she said nothing directly related to Janet Taber and company, I knew she was trying to fill in some of the holes for me.

An uncle of theirs, she said, had worked for Simon Norman from the thirties up until ten years ago. This uncle was usually referred to in the family as the "rich" uncle, since he had by far the best-paying job of any family member. When the uncle had to leave the position due to failing health (he was sixty-five at the time and died within the year), he recommended his nephew Harold to Simon Norman as his replacement. Even though Harold's background was a trifle rough (he *had* lost his eye in a gang-fight as a kid, just as Jack Masters had told me), he had covered, in a five-year period of bumming around, a number of jobs that seemed applicable to the position: he had been everything from nightclub bouncer to gardener to short-order cook to hospital orderly, and the only duty of the uncle's he couldn't take on officially was that of chauffeur, since he couldn't get a chauffeur's license due to his missing eye; but unofficially he was up to it, and Norman rarely went out these days, anyway.

When Norman gave him the job on a trial basis, Harold made an immediate effort to live up to his "rich" uncle's image, an effort that helped fill the long hours in the empty old house. He began a self-education program, by reading, and, later, through correspondence courses of many kinds. While he had grown intellectually since beginning to work for Norman, he had become increasingly isolated and somewhat arrested socially—or so Rita felt. She said that even his irregular visits up to different clubs in the Quad Cities—where among other blacks he would revert somewhat to his rougher, less reserved old self—had stopped a year or so ago, when Norman had a severe stroke. And he rarely if ever went out into Port City even on errands, having everything delivered, and only once in a great while would he drive up to Rock Island to see Rita. He'd had for a time a steady woman in the Cities, but broke it off shortly after Norman's stroke.

I lost patience sucking and bit down on the Lifesaver. I chewed it up and swallowed. I had kind of a raw taste in my mouth, combination of sour, from not brushing my teeth for a decade or so, and sweet, from chewed-up Lifesaver. I got up to get a drink of water.

Even though I hadn't been sleeping, it took me a moment to get my balance. I stretched my back, felt the spinal knuckles pop, and suddenly was very awake, even more awake than is usual in my occasional insomniac turns. I decided I was awake enough to have more than a glass of water, ready for a glass of orange juice, maybe. I made my way to the kitchenette, my eyes so well-adjusted to the dark I stubbed not a single toe, and opened up the icebox and got out a bottle of Pabst.

I went over to the couch and sat staring at my front door, drinking my Pabst, feet on the coffee table, feeling, about halfway through my beer, tired for the first time that night. My eyes were getting fuzzy and the lids were drooping and I almost thought for a second I could see the door knob moving. Turning.

Well, boy, when inanimate objects start moving around, then you know you're falling asleep, or already asleep and dreaming, and I was about to let my lids slide all the way shut when the door opened, all the way, and I was awake again.

I didn't move.

It was dark. Whoever it was wouldn't expect me to be up, wide awake, eyes in tune with the darkness.

He was big. The outline of him as he stood in the doorway was huge, shoulders almost touching the frame of the door. But I couldn't see who it was, it was just a massive black form in the door, the light very bright around the shape, from the streetlamps and the piece of moon now out from behind the clouds.

I stayed motionless. I was sure he didn't see me. He was putting something in his pocket now, the skeleton key he'd used to get in, maybe, or maybe some gizmo he'd picked the lock with.

One thing I knew: it wasn't John, or even Brennan, or anybody else friendly or semi-friendly who might be playing a practical joke. He was too big even for Brennan, too wide, and the slow, methodical way he moved had no humor in it at all, just deadly, serious business.

He stepped inside and shut the door gently behind him and lifted a hand with a long-shafted flashlight in it. He switched on the flash and aimed it over toward where the living room trails into the hall that leads into the bedroom.

I slipped my feet down off the coffee table. Like I was balancing an egg on each toe.

He directed the flash down the hall, moving toward there himself, his free hand balled into a fist that was like a rock he was getting ready to pound into somebody's head.

I threw the beer bottle at him and caught him on the ear.

He fell against the wall and slid down, the flash rolling out of his grasp, and I jumped through the darkness at him and caught a knee in my stomach. I tumbled away and smacked into the coffee table and then crawled off to catch my breath, but I could hear him scrambling around behind me.

He wasn't used to the dark like I was, and he didn't know where the light switch was, to do something about it. I hustled off on my hands and knees toward the kitchenette while he was rustling around after the flashlight, which had got switched off when he fumbled it.

Then the beam of the flash started cutting through the room's darkness like the searching strokes of a knife. I huddled in the corner of the kitchenette, my mind stuttering. I edged my hand up the woodwork and over into the sink and my fingers found a glass, and then the skillet, still greasy from the American fries. I brought both skillet and glass, carefully, soundlessly, out of the sink and down to me, clutching them to me like treasure. I hefted the skillet; it wasn't as heavy as I would've liked, but it was iron and it would do. I watched the probing beam of light, then aimed as best I could and pitched the glass at him and knocked the flash from his hand, then crouched with the iron pan in hand and waited for him to come after me.

Light filled the room.

Rita stood at the mouth of the hall, her hand on the light switch. She presented quite a sight: a beautiful naked brown girl with tousled black hair and brown nipples and . . .

And he was a big white guy and he stood and looked at her with his mouth hanging open.

In that second he gave me, I crowned him from behind with the skillet.

For a big man, he went down fast, hitting his cheekbone as he fell, and it wasn't necessary to clobber him again. Rita came rushing over, questions tumbling out of her, but I snapped an order at her, telling her to get me a tie out of my closet, and she jiggled out after it and back with it in four seconds flat. I quickly bound his hands behind him, but there was nothing to worry about: he wasn't anywhere near conscious yet.

I flipped him over. Well, he was too heavy to flip, really, alone anyway: I needed Rita's help to do it, as out of breath as I was.

"What's this all about, Mal?" she wanted to know. She was so startled by all of this she wasn't bothering to cover up; I was so startled I wasn't bothering to look.

"I'm not sure myself," I said. "But it's safe to say this guy wanted to do some damage."

Then, as an afterthought, I searched him quickly and found a small, compact automatic. Blue metal, pearl-handled, it looked like the kind of thing women sometimes carry in purses. I balanced it in my palm.

Rita looked at the gun and swallowed. "What are you gonna do now?"

"I'm going to call my friend John and get him and his hardass stepfather over here. I'll be damned if that sonofabitch Brennan is going to ignore *this*."

"Should I get some clothes on?"

I grinned. "Well, it'd make John's day if you didn't, but I don't think Brennan's ready for it."

She grinned back and covered herself rather demurely, like *September Morn*, but I wasn't completely buying it. "You swing a mean skillet," she said.

"You swing a mean . . . go get in your clothes."

I went over to the phone and dialed.

John answered, groggily.

"Thanksgiving's over," I said. "Drag Brennan out of bed and get him over here.

Somebody just broke into my place and I had to hit him with a skillet."

"Huh?"

I told him again and he got it this time. I added that though I hadn't hit the guy hard enough to kill him or anything, I'd done a good enough job that a doctor would probably be a wise thing to bring along.

"Who is it? That black guy with one eye?"

"Hardly."

"Well, then who the hell is he? You ever see him before?"

"Yeah," I said, looking over at the still slumbering housebreaker. He was wearing a yellow sweater and mustard bell-bottoms. "His name is Davis."

PART FOUR

NOVEMBER 29, 1974

FRIDAY

TWENTY-ONE

I stood outside the hospital room and leaned back against the wall; its tile surface was cold on my neck. Down the hall a few feet, by the elevator, Brennan was shuffling around the small waiting area, giving the "No Smoking" sign a dirty look each time he passed. He kept turning the brim of his Stetson in his hands like a piece of evidence he couldn't make anything out of. Then he wandered over to one of the windows opposite the elevator and stared out at the morning blackness.

I left him alone. Went over and sat on a couch. I was just too damn tired to play the I-told-you-so-I-told-you-so game. And Brennan was boiling, anyway—why get him any angrier? It was hard to tell whether his irritation was because of my digging into this when it was none of my business, or if it was just because nobody is crazy about getting rousted out of bed in the wee morning hours. And, as he pointed out a number of times, I really should've called the Port City police instead of him.

But he *had* come out himself, and as yet hadn't contacted the Port City cops. Which gave me at least some reason to stay a shade wary of his motives.

I yawned. In my head, my eyes were stones. A few minutes crawled by and Brennan drew away from the window and began pacing in front of the couch like an expectant father.

The couch was in a waiting area facing the elevator door, which I was staring at, Brennan's form cutting my path of vision as he went by. Several minutes more dragged past, and I started nodding off, then got startled awake as the elevator door slid away like an effect in a cheap science-fiction movie. John was standing there with three Pepsi necks in the tortured grasp of one hand and a box of doughnuts in the other. He came over and sat beside me on the couch adjacent to mine, and handed me over the box of doughnuts while he put the Pepsis safely down on the floor. Brennan immediately forgot his mad and joined the communal feed.

There were two doughnuts apiece, and I was finishing my first and Brennan was starting his second when he said, through a mouthful, "This Davis."

John and I looked up at him and I said, "What?"

Brennan repeated, "This Davis," and swallowed the bite of doughnut.

"Yeah," I said, "go on."

"I know him."

"How do you happen to know him?"

"Know of him's more like it."

"Where do you know him from?"

"The Cities. He's been involved in some things up there."

"What kind of things?"

"Oh, you know, strong-arm stuff. Putting pressure on people."

"He goes around putting pressure on people."

"Yeah."

"Why does he do that, Brennan?"

"That's what he does, that's all. That's his living. Some people didn't inherit money, Mallory. Some people got to go out and turn a buck, which is something you wouldn't know much about."

"What you're trying to say is he's a thug."

Brennan shrugged.

"A thug for the Normans," I added.

"I didn't say that. The stuff I heard about Davis dates back to when he was working for some mob guys in the Cities."

"What mob guys in the Cities? I never heard about any mob guys in the Cities."

"There's gambling up there, isn't there?

Anyway, Davis has been in and out of the frying pan, mostly in, and lost his job with his previous employers for fumbling the ball once too often."

"When did Davis start working for the Normans?"

"Look, that's an idea *you* got, not something either one of us knows for a fact."

"What was he doing with Stefan Norman yesterday?"

"From what you told me, he was eating turkey."

"Come on."

"All I know is if Davis ever did do work for the Normans, it would've been back when Richard was running for office—you know, running for Congress."

"Why do you say that?"

"Well, they were having some trouble keeping some of the garbage about old Simon from out of the papers. You know the press. Trying to do a smear job on Richard by using the old man's record against the son. Really dirty tactics."

"Really dirty tactics. I hope Davis straightened everybody out."

"Listen, Mallory, this is nothing I'm sure about, this is just something I put together in my head."

"Why are you being so helpful all of a sudden?"

"No reason."

"Gee, I almost forgot what a nice guy you are."

Brennan drained the remaining half of his Pepsi in one monumental series of gulps, then shrugged. He said, "All right, Mallory, I'll give it to you straight. I mean, you're my son's friend and I guess I been a little down on you at times, so I'll level with you once and for all. You were right the other day, I *have* been doing some . . . well . . . coverin' up for the Normans."

John dropped the final quarter of his doughnut and it rolled on the floor. He looked at his stepfather with open disgust.

Brennan's face twisted, turned away from his stepson. "Hell, don't everybody go all righteous on me, all of a sudden. Nobody's making me tell you any of this."

"Go ahead," I said.

"Nothing to go ahead with. The Normans still got their share of pull in these parts, and that's the whole story right there. Sure, they haven't been so active since Richard died, but even now their people control county politics, it's Norman money behind it all. Norman people got to okay the candidates, before they provide campaign money. Simple as that. How do you think I stayed sheriff as long as I have? Here I am, an elected official, still in office after more than twelve years."

"But it's a Republican county," John said, "always has been. You wouldn't ever've had any trouble getting elected, not when that's the ticket you run on anyway."

"First you got to get *on* the ticket, son. This ain't Republican or Democrat, it's politics. And I told you, Norman people control the politics in this county."

I said, "And in return the Normans expect an occasional favor."

"That's right. No big deal."

"No big deal," John said, flatly. "Just small stuff, like covering up murders."

"Aw, can the murder crap. Where do you get that from? All it was, was Stefan Norman said, you know, just look the other way a little on this Janet Taber deal. He explained it to me, how the girl had some kind of blackmail scheme cooked up, only it didn't pan out, and then she ran herself off Colorado Hill, out of, you know, remorse. Stefan said a lot of noise over the girl's death might drag in the Norman name and things could get blown out of proportion, so . . ." He shrugged again; he seemed embarrassed.

"What was Janet Taber blackmailing them over?" I asked.

He pointed a thick finger at me. "I know for a fact that was just a damn hoax. Something she cooked up outa whole cloth. I know the details."

"What *are* the details?"

"I gave my word I wouldn't reveal them."

"You gave your word to Stefan, you mean."

"Don't ask me to say more. At least not at this time."

John said, "Don't push him on it, Mal. Can't you see he's a man of principle?"

Brennan ignored the sarcasm. He said, "I just want you to know, Mallory, John, that I'll handle this thing from here on out. You were right, Mallory—I was wrong: there probably was foul play of some kind, where the Taber girl was concerned. But now that I'm in, *you're* out."

"And you'll start," I said, "with Stefan Norman sending Davis after me?"

"Who says Stefan sent him?"

"Oh, Brennan."

"Seems to me you assume a hell of a lot, Mallory. That's why your half-ass investigation hasn't got too far."

"See to it yours doesn't amount to you just looking the other way some more."

"It won't," Brennan said, and he slapped his knees like a department store Santa summoning the next kid. "I see it this way: if the Normans got some secrets they want kept that way, well fine. But when those secrets start including crimes, like breaking and entering into your place, and I'll grant you that Taber girl's death is looking fishy in hindsight, well then . . ." And he paused to flash a big grin, ". . . then I'll have to slap on my shit-kicking boots, boys."

If that was meant to make me feel warm inside, it didn't. And Brennan hadn't endeared himself to his stepson, either: John's face had drained of color and his eyes were cold.

Down the hall the door to Davis's room opened and the three of us stood up and watched the doctor walk down to us. He was around thirty, of medium height and had sandy, longish hair and wireframe glasses. He carried an aluminum clipboard, carried it like it was heavy, like he'd rather be anywhere at that moment than in a hospital in Port City, Iowa, at three in the morning.

"Can I have him now, doc?" Brennan said.

"Better we keep him here," he said.

"Something serious?" Brennan gave me a quick sideways glare.

"No, doubt there's much chance of that. Probably a mild concussion is all, though we'll need a closer look."

I said, "Can I talk to him?"

"You can try," he said. "That is, if it's agreeable with the sheriff. But you probably won't have much luck."

"Why's that?" Brennan asked, shifting foot to foot.

"Well," the doctor sighed, "that is one of the primary reasons it's best we keep him at least overnight. You see, he is conscious, but he won't say a word. You can talk away at him but he won't respond whatsoever."

"What do you make of it?" I said. "Shock?"

"Amnesia?" Brennan chimed in.

The doctor chuckled and said, "Doubtful, though he may indeed be trying to simulate memory loss, for some kind of effect; that is, assuming he's seen the same soap operas and old movies you have, Sheriff."

"If he's just faking . . ." Brennan said, moving forward.

The doctor held out his hand in a stop gesture. "Check back with us this afternoon. In the meantime, you'll want to send someone to guard his room."

Brennan nodded.

The doctor nodded back, then turned and walked off.

Brennan said, "I better go down and phone the chief of police and have him send a man over. This is going to have to be a cooperative investigation anyway, might as well take advantage of the situation." He turned to John and said, "Keep an eye on Davis till I get back." He looked at me and then back at John and said, "And keep *his* butt out of that room, okay? Keep in mind *I'm* handling this from now on, son."

We watched Brennan walk to the elevator, disappear inside. When he was gone, John stared poker-faced after him. Then he jerked his thumb toward Davis's room.

"Go on down there and see what you can get out of him."

Davis was staring at the ceiling, his hospital bed completely flat. His long arms lay in front of him like the branches of a dead tree; his flesh was nearly as white as the hospital gown. There was not a flicker of recognition in his face as I approached, no trace of anything, except a deep purple bruise on one cheek. On top of his head, however, in the nest of thinning, dyed-blond hair was the goose egg my frying pan had produced. That was the only thing remotely comic about Davis, however: otherwise you'd have to put a mirror to his lips and see the fog before attesting to his being alive.

"Davis."

I cranked the bed into a sitting position and his eyes remained open and staring. Motionless.

"Davis," I said, "why did you break into my place?"

It was like trying to communicate with a figure in a wax museum. His face stayed expressionless, his eyes didn't move. Didn't twitch. Didn't blink.

"What did Stefan want done to me, Davis? Did he want me dead?"

Didn't move. Didn't twitch. Didn't blink.

"Did you kill Janet Taber, Davis? Did Stefan ask you to do that?"

Didn't move. Didn't twitch. Didn't blink.

"Did you break her neck with your hands? She didn't have a very big neck. Did you pour booze all over her car and put her inside and push it off Colorado Hill? Did you do all that, Davis?"

Didn't move. Didn't twitch. Didn't blink.

"I'm going to find out," I said. "You tell Stefan when he comes with flowers. If Stefan doesn't show, tell the lawyer he sends, tell him to tell Stefan."

Then he moved. Twitched. Blinked.

Crooked a finger and motioned for me to come closer.

I stayed where I was.

He spoke and it was just a whisper, like a guy with terminal laryngitis. I couldn't make out a damn thing he was saying.

I leaned in a bit and his big hands reached out and clutched my neck.

And squeezed.

He was strong, Christ was he strong. Those hands had only been on my throat a few seconds and already the world was turning red-fading-to-black, but somehow I found the strength, and the sense, to throw a punch into him, into his chest, a pretty damn good hard right hand, considering the strain I was under.

Since he was still in bed, and at an awkward position to maintain a stranglehold, the punch was enough to send him back and his hands, thank God!, went with him.

But not for long. They both lashed out at me, fists now, and I felt my face go to the right and then to the left, like I was slapped, twice, by a two-by-four.

I was on my butt, then, sitting with my head in my hands, vaguely aware that Davis was lumbering out of bed and toward the door; from the sound of it, he was moving fast, and awkwardly. I glanced up and my eyes focused and saw him go out, hospital gown flapping, slamming the door behind him, only it closed hospital soft.

I tried to yell out, but my throat hurt; there was no sound there to come out. I pushed up, got onto my feet and went to the door myself, to warn John.

But John didn't need warning.

Halfway down the hall, on his way to the elevators, Davis had been met by John, and the two faced each other in crouches; John's crouch spoke of martial arts training—Davis's spoke of single-minded brute force.

I wanted to come up behind Davis and put an end to this—who the hell needed a fair fight when a lummox like him was involved?—only my head was whirling and when I went to move fast, I stumbled and fell to my knees. Those two punches I'd taken from Davis—and the choke-hold—had done a number on me.

In a way, though, that was enough to help John.

Because Davis heard me, and turned his head to see what it was, and John karate-kicked him in the stomach, sending Davis backward and sitting him down on the cold corridor floor.

It had been a quiet fight so far; no doctors or nurses, and certainly no patients, had come running.

That was about to change.

Davis got up and ran barreling toward John, making a sound like a wounded, pissed-off buffalo, and even karate couldn't stop that beast, in that confined a space. He plowed a blocklike shoulder and head into John, and John went skidding down the floor into some of the furniture in the reception area by the elevators.

Before John could get up, backed up against a sofa by a window, Davis was bending over him, pummeling him with rocklike fists, and I was finally stumbling down toward them, so I could get into this, and I hoped to put a quick stop to it. That doctor I'd seen earlier was coming up behind me—I could hear his voice: "Stop this! Stop it!"—and some nurses were bringing up the rear, though that I couldn't see at the moment.

And then before I or the doctor or anybody else could put a stop to it, John did.

He'd taken half a dozen vicious fists in

the body and face when he thrust a leg up, straight up into Davis's belly and hurled Davis up and over and toward the window just behind that sofa John was backed against.

And whether it was what John had in mind or not, I can't say—and he never told me, because I never asked—but Davis went sailing through that window, taking a curtain and venetian blinds with him, and the shattering glass rained down on John and he shielded his eyes as it did.

Davis didn't scream, but he made a thud, three stories down.

I helped John up—his eyes were wide but not wild—and he rushed to the window, putting a hand less carefully than he should on the jagged teeth of glass as he looked out.

Davis was sprawled on his stomach, tangled in the curtain and blinds; a motionless white splotch against the dark ground.

"Let's get down there," John said.

The doctor was just reaching the window as John and I got on the elevator; we went down alone, and were out to Davis before any of the hospital staff.

John leaned over him, felt for his pulse on his neck; but we both knew the man was gone—his blood-flecked face had its eyes open in the stare of the dead.

John stood up and walked across the

hospital lawn and stood and stared at nothing in particular; I followed. Both of us were bleeding a little, from the punishment Davis had dished out on us. Behind us the doctor and a couple of orderlies rushed to the body.

I stood there with him; put a hand on his shoulder.

He turned and smiled at me. Not his dazzler: a tight-lipped, sad smile.

"See, Mal?" he said. "It doesn't matter."

"What?"

"Where you go," he said.

"What do you mean?"

He shrugged. "You sure don't need to go to Vietnam."

"What?"

"You don't have to go there to find it," he said.

"What are you talking about?"

He looked older to me then than anybody that young ever looked, except maybe for Janet Taber.

"What are you talking about?" I repeated.

"Killing," he said. "Death."

Pretty soon Brennan showed with some local cops and we gave him our statements while the emergency room doctor looked us over and cleaned and dressed the places where we bled.

TWENTY-TWO

I got back to my trailer around four-thirty and found Rita up, stirring around in the kitchenette. She was wearing a stretched out old Iowa sweatshirt of mine that hit her mid-thigh like a miniskirt, and normally I'd have spent some time wondering what she had on under there, only I was too burned out to really care. I had called her from the hospital an hour or so ago, to warn her I'd be late—and to tell her about Davis's fall. As I walked across the living room I tripped over the empty beer bottle I'd tossed at Davis and the bottle seemed an apt metaphor for how I felt: empty, useless, nonreturnable.

Rita said, "I couldn't sleep."

"I haven't been up this late since junior-senior prom."

"No offense, but you look like shit, honey."

"Guess how I feel."

"Like you look."

"Like I look," I confirmed, stumbling over to the couch where I flopped down on my stomach. My nose sniffed the air: something nice cooking. I said, "What smells good?"

Rita said, "I found a coffee cake mix in your cupboard. I'm making it. Is that okay?"

"That's not okay. That's wonderful. What else do I smell?"

"Coffee to go with it, stupid."

"How long till the coffee cake?"

"Few minutes."

"How long till the coffee?"

"Right now."

"Hot damn." I rolled over on my back—the dying dog's last trick. I pulled the flesh away from my eyes with the flats of my hands, then got started on a series of overlapping yawns.

Rita came over bearing coffee. Good hot steam rose off the liquid in the cup and I inhaled it, then sipped. She nudged herself room next to me on the couch. Her big brown eyes were open wide as she said, "Are you okay?"

"Yeah," I said. "I don't know how John's doing, though."

"Why?"

"I think it disturbed him, having this sort of thing happen in . . . the civilian world."

"Oh."

"Too bad it went the way it did. Davis is no great loss to humanity, I suppose, but he took a lot of information with him." I sipped the coffee. "You know, Brennan came out and admitted he's been sweeping the case under the carpet for the Normans."

"No shit?"

"None at all. I'll say this much for him: it took a certain quota of guts just to admit it."

She made a face. "Oh, please."

"He's an S.O.B., all right, I won't argue with you there. But even a belated stand against the Normans could cost the sheriff his job. I just hope he doesn't go overboard trying to make up for lost time. You know, going into a gestapo number."

"Coffee cake."

"Huh?"

"The coffee cake should be done."

"But I got some brilliant deductions to share with you."

"If I don't take it out it'll burn." And she rose and bounded toward the kitchenette.

I said, "I know who killed Janet Taber."

"Tell me over the coffee cake," she said, opening the oven door.

"Sheesh," I said. "I solve the mystery and nobody gives a damn."

The coffee cake was very good, moist and yellow and rich with crunchy cinnamon topping and my mouth surrounded a piece as Rita said, "Well, don't pout. Spill!"

I spoke with my mouth full. "I don't have any of the details figured out, understand. I mean, the pieces don't form a picture yet or anything."

"So who did it, already?"

"Davis did it, no doubt in my mind."

"Why?"

"Because Stefan Norman told him to."

"Why?"

"I think because Janet had something on the Normans. Maybe something she ran across back when she was working on Richard Norman's campaign team."

"What about Harold?"

She flipped the question out casually, lightly, like the rest of her conversation, but unlike the rest of it, this didn't float: it was a leaden lump in her throat even after spoken.

I said, "Don't worry. Your brother's in the clear. I'm as sure of that as I am of Stefan's guilt."

She couldn't hold back her sigh of relief, but she tried to cover it by sipping her coffee right after.

"You know," I said, "your brother's a nice man."

"I could've told you that."

"You did. Several times."

"Now that you've ruled my brother out, I suppose you're through with me. Won't be needing my services anymore. Shove my black butt right out your door."

"Oh, I don't know. I could use a sleep-in maid around here."

"Oh, typecasting, is it?"

"Maybe. Only I think of you more as the French maid type."

She smiled and flicked a crumb of coffee cake at me and it landed on my nose. I brushed it away and leaned over and kissed her.

We were lying together kind of half asleep on the couch when the phone rang.

"Yeah?"

"Mal?"

"John, why in hell are *you* still up? Are you all right?"

"I went back to bed for a while, couldn't sleep. Then the phone rang."

"So who called?"

"The nightwatchman at the Maxwell Building."

"The nightwatchman at the Maxwell Building. Well, what did the nightwatchman at the Maxwell Building have to say?"

"Nothing to me, Mal. It was Brennan's call."

"What about?"

"Swing by the jail and pick me up, will you? We'll go over there and you can see. Brennan's there with the cops now."

"What the hell is it?"

"Stefan Norman's been shot."

TWENTY-THREE

"Suicide," Brennan said.

I said nothing.

I looked at the desk where a few minutes prior the husk of Stefan Norman had been sitting. Stefan's desk was big and black and metallic, with a small white blotter in its center, a throw rug on a ballroom floor. The blotter where Stefan's head must have rested had a wine-color stain that had blossomed out, suggesting hidden shapes and meanings in Rorschach fashion. Otherwise the desk was bare, except for the blood-red push-button phone, and a small black automatic, responsible for the smell of cordite in the air.

Stefan's office was large and the lack of furniture made it seem larger. The desk with one brown leather chair behind it and another opposite and a couch along the draped window-wall were like the last props waiting to be cleared off the set of a play that had closed. Not that this indicated the Norman Fund was a dummy operation: the outer office had rows of file cabinets and all the standard equipment, including a photocopy machine and the work-heaped desks of two full-time secretaries. And beyond that was a reception area complete with stacks of old *U.S. News and World Report*s. The Norman Fund had indeed been functioning at something or other.

I was feeling a little bit shook: deaths aren't an everyday thing for me, not yet anyway, not even after everyday contact with them, which I've had from time to time, everything from typing obits all morning for a newspaper to tromping through some poor Asian guy's rice crop with a rifle in my hands.

Also, I felt cheated: I didn't have a chance to know Stefan Norman, let alone understand him. He was just a guy I talked to once for a few minutes; yet a guy who was important to me, a guy whose head I wanted to climb inside of to find the answers to some questions. A port of entry was there now, all right, but not for climbing in—for seepage only. The things in there, the man in there, were lost.

And, too, I had the spooky feeling that I was walking through a slightly altered replay of the events of Tuesday evening past. First off, John showed up in the yellow fringed buckskin jacket, blue shirt and black leather pants he'd worn then, but there was a logical reason for that: now that he'd soured on his stepfather, John was digging out his most outlandish outfits to make Brennan as uncomfortable as possible. Then at the Maxwell Building we were momentarily stopped by Oliver DeForest, the same guy who stopped us out at Colorado Hill Tuesday night. Next, John and I stood waiting for the elevator to come down and who should the doors open up on but Tuesday night's ambulance boys, only this time it wasn't Janet's body they were cheerfully hauling out, but Stefan's. I looked at John and said, "Déjà vu," and he said, "Gesundheit."

Brennan said, "Don't touch anything."

I motioned to the couch. "Mind if I sit down?"

"Be my guest."

I walked over to the couch and John followed. We sat and watched Brennan and a cop in uniform and another in a baggy gray suit wander around and try to find something to do. The uniformed cop asked Brennan if somebody ought to take fingerprints and Brennan said why bother. The guy in the baggy suit said what about the gun and Brennan said he was sure it was Stefan's but check it out anyway and go ahead and take it down and get it checked for prints. Gray suit went over to the desk and shoved a pencil down the automatic's barrel and walked to the door carrying the gun-on-a-pencil like a boy scout carrying Old Glory in the parade. As he opened the door, the gun started to slide off the pencil and he instinctively guided it back in place with his free hand; he passed the torch to a cop who for no particular reason was standing watch in the outer office and told him what to do and came back and wandered around some more. The uniformed cop said anybody see the shell casing and Brennan said he already picked it up. It went on like that for fifteen minutes.

Finally I said, "Can I talk to you for a second, Brennan?"

Brennan said, "I'm kinda busy."

"Are you?"

"Okay, okay, go ahead and talk."

"Can we have some privacy?"

"Jesus, Mallory!"

"Brennan?"

"Let's go on out in the hall, then."

I looked at John and said, "Coming?"

He shook his head no. "You talk to him."

Brennan and I walked out through the two outer offices and stood by the elevators, no one else around. "Private enough?" he said.

I said, "Suicide?"

"That's right. Cut and dried."

"Now isn't that convenient?"

"What? Just what do you mean?"

"Just that it's a nice, safe way to end the affair. For all concerned."

"What are you implying, Mallory?"

"Am I implying something?"

"Okay, mystery writer," Brennan said, punching the down button, "you come with me, I wanna show you something."

We rode down in the elevator without a word, walked quickly past DeForest and went directly to Brennan's Buick, parked in front of the building. Brennan unlocked the car door and reached in the front seat for a manila folder. He took a sheet of paper from the folder, carefully holding it by one corner with thumb and middle finger, and gave it to me, instructing me to hold it the same way.

"Read it," he said.

"What is it?"

"What do you think it is?"

I read it over quickly, then said, "This is supposed to be a suicide note?"

"Not supposed to be. *Is.*"

"Have you checked the handwriting out?"

"I know Stefan Norman's handwriting, and that's it."

"But you are going to have an expert check it, aren't you?"

"The P.D.'ll handle that end of it. That's

up to them. I suppose they'll check it out, but just as a formality. Take my word, that's Stefan Norman's handwriting all right. You wanna hand that back now?"

"No, give me a second, I want to reread it."

I went over it again, more slowly this time. It was written out longhand, in a style tight, cramped and somehow delicate. It said:

I, Stefan Norman, am responsible for the deaths of Janet Taber and her mother, Renata Ferris. I felt I was working in the best interests of myself, my family and the Fund. I was in grave error.

It was my belief that Mrs. Taber and her mother, Mrs. Ferris, were attempting to blackmail certain members of my family.

In the pursuit of this belief, I approached Mrs. Ferris on the subject of her daughter's conduct, only to find reason to suspect the mother's complicity in her daughter's action. The last of several arguments resulted in a physical confrontation. She (Mrs. Ferris) was a big woman and in the heat of the moment, attacked my person.

I retaliated and she was badly injured. In panic, I left the house. Later, by accident I presume, a fire began. In this indirect manner, I am responsible for her death.

George Davis killed Janet Taber, acting on a misinterpretation of a request of mine that she be asked to leave Port City at once. In this way, I am responsible for her death—and Davis's, as well, indirectly.

I realize now my mistake in regard to Janet Taber and her mother and have deep feelings of sorrow and regret over the entire matter.

It was signed "Stefan H. Norman," and dated.

I handed the page back to Brennan and he took it, easing it gently into the manila folder. He leaned inside the car, laid the folder on the seat and then locked it back up. He turned to me and said, "Answers a lot of questions, doesn't it?"

I said nothing.

TWENTY-FOUR

Dawn. The sun glanced off the smooth surfaces of the Norman house, ricocheted off its sharp edges and shot blinding crossfires of glare across our eyes as Rita and I approached in the Rambler. The house looked smaller in the light of day, as though someone had come in during the night and replaced it with a scale model; and while no less grotesque in the morning light, the art deco castle seemed somehow less frightening, like a ghost that in the turning on of a light is revealed as a sheet caught on a nail.

We got out of the Rambler and I stood and had a look at the place. The slabs of interlocking cement showed a fresh crack here and there, as well as patches of mortarwork where others had been; the house just didn't lend itself to mint preservation. Oh, if nobody tore it down, it'd be standing in a hundred years or two, but all that concrete, unpainted like it was, was bound to chip and crumble and lose some of its shape and, well, beauty. As a relic to be found in ages to come, by intergalactic free-booters perhaps, or maybe the mutated remains of whatever becomes of our race, the Norman place'll be an enigmatic curiosity piece that, like a sunbleached skull sticking up out of the desert sand, makes one wonder what story was behind it.

Harold filled the back doorway. He was wearing a gray suit, white shirt open at the collar. He made like a cigar store Indian for a few moments, then came to partial life and motioned us in, grimly.

Rita gave me a look that included a quick downward movement of the mouth, which I took as meaning she was worried about just how bad I'd screwed up her relationship with her brother.

I gave her a look that said, come off it, it's six in the morning, a couple hours after the violent death of one of his employers, how do you *expect* him to act?

And she sighed and let go a tentative smile. Very tentative.

Harold was about to usher us into his room, saying something about getting us some coffee. I quickly stated the purpose of my visit, hoping to avoid any further amenities: I apologized for implying that he might've been involved in Janet Taber's death, and said I was sorry for any inconvenience I might have caused either him or Mr. Norman. And I expressed my sympathy for the loss of Stefan. Then I asked if I might go up and express the same sentiments to Mr. Norman.

Harold's one eye narrowed on me a good long while. There was, I thought, skepticism in that eye, along with it being bloodshot. He was absolutely still, staring at me, like a freeze-frame in a film, then said, "You can go on up, Mallory."

"Thanks, Harold."

"But don't wake him if he's got back to sleep, though I don't imagine he will have."

"I won't."

"And don't upset him."

"I won't."

"Then go on up."

"Thanks."

Norman was in his wheelchair. He had wheeled himself over a tiny ramp that led up to the desk on the stagelike platform. He sat at the desk looking out the long viewscreen of a window that faced the river.

"Sir," I said.

He turned his head slightly, but not enough, I thought, for him to see me. Just the same, he said, "Oh, hello, young man. I'm glad you've come back to continue our chat."

"I'm glad you're glad."

"I'm not really in any better spirits than before—perhaps even a shade worse—but I don't anticipate getting quite as cantankerous as I did toward the end there last time you were up. Damn old people, anyway, changing their mind before it's made up the first time. Please forgive my rudeness."

"Only if you'll forgive mine," I said. "For breaking in on you the way I did."

"I enjoyed your company," he said, still facing away from me, toward the river. "Come join me here, would you? The view is very nice here, share it with me, please."

I walked across the long empty room glancing at the portrait in purple over the fireplace, and stepped up on the platform and looked out the window. The sun was still rising, the sky was gray, and rose-gray just over the line of trees, which had the artificial, nearly surreal appearance of a landscape painted by one of your relatives. Not a beautiful sunrise, rather an eerie one, unreal, a collaboration between Grandma Moses and Salvador Dali, and I wondered if sunrises always looked that way from the Norman house.

I had almost said, "Quite a sunrise," when Norman said, "Right down there it was," and I suddenly realized he wasn't watching the sun come up at all, his head was tilted downward, toward the lawn that stretched for a hundred yards or so from the house to the edge of the bluff. He was staring at the dead brown grass, pointing a trembling finger.

He said, "There used to be flowers all around, bordering that lawn, and the lawn was green. The country club with its golf course would have liked to have grass so lush and green and rich. Every Sunday they'd gather there, folks from all over, they'd drive here and come sit out on the lawn and just look up at the building. Some were sick and needed help, others . . . others just liked to hear, well, as I used to call it, the 'Sound of Truth'—that was what my Sunday broadcast was called. So anyway, what was it you asked? Oh, the gathering on the lawn. Well they came from all over and filled the parking lot, which took up all the space and more than that supermarket 'cross the street does now, the one by that filling station that stands where mine used to. And they'd sit out on the grass and we'd pump the broadcast out to them over speakers and would they ever listen. We put tents up in dreary weather, 'cause a little rain wouldn't keep them away from Doc Sy Norman and Station KTKO and the Sound of Truth."

He shook his head and a lock of the long white hair fell like a thick comma across his brow; the blue hypnotist's eyes were open and clear and you could see they'd been compelling in their day. "You know,

it made you feel . . . important. Hell, I *was*
important, and I *knew* it, and I was doing
people good, too, no matter what some
thought and said. Do you know that? I *did*
do people good, and I've done good since,
in different ways, quieter ways. I've helped
this town, it's grown because of me, people
have jobs because of me, they feed their
families, do you know that? Did you know
I licked the scoundrels who ran the water
'n' light trust? It was *me* got a municipal
water and light plant put up, back in '26.
And that building's still in use today. You go
look at it. I designed it, just like I designed
this house. And like this house it'll be
there long after I'm gone. Did you know I
drew the rough design of this house on a
tablecloth? Well it's true. The night we got
the okay from the Department of Com-
merce, you know, to go ahead and build
the station, well a bunch of us got together
in my café and started trying to pin down
this hazy aircastle I'd been dreaming of so
long. Everybody had an idea of his own of
what it should be and just about every
kind of architecture you can think of got
suggested. Then it came to me . . . why not
take the best of all of them and build
something unique? A touch of Spanish
here, a dab of Egyptian there, and toss in
some of what that man Wright was doing.
And I built it here, on the highest point in
Port City, two hundred feet above the

Mississippi, where everyone, always, could see it. And years from now they'll say, that's Doc Sy's hill and that's where he lived and worked, and when I'm long gone it'll still be up here. You know, a man likes knowing he's left something behind that'll be there after he's gone, you know that?"

"It must be a comforting feeling," I said, "to know you've accomplished something in your life."

"Oh it is, it is indeed. Though, I'll tell you, uh, what was your name?"

"Mallory."

"Mallory. I'll tell you, Mallory, a man feels a little empty at this stage of life, no matter how full it's been up to then. It's a kind of a used-up feeling, I guess, and it doesn't matter how grand your achievements . . ." (he affectionately patted the glass over the autographed picture of Hoover) ". . . no matter how grand, you just feel empty."

I didn't say anything; it would've been a good time to find things out, but I couldn't make myself ask anything.

Finally, he went on himself: "It's not so much I miss her—my wife, I mean—it's been so long ago, and she was a young girl and here I am an old man, but . . . I don't have anything left of her and there won't be anything left of her after I'm gone . . . nothing of the two of us together . . . not with Richard gone . . . and my grandson."

His mind must've been wandering, I thought; Stefan was his nephew, not his grandson.

He went on: "... and Stefan, too, is a loss, I suppose, even if I do feel some bitterness, can't help but feel some bitterness...."

I had to say something now. Inside me I sealed compassion over, much as someone had mortared the cracks in the old house.

I said, "I suppose you must feel a little bit sad, being the last of the Normans. It's a lot of tragedy to go through, losing a wife, a son and his wife and daughter, and now your nephew."

"He shouldn't have done it."

"Commit suicide you mean?"

"No, no, boy, that's not at all what I mean. Under the circumstances suicide was ideal, really. It's that he shouldn't have gone bothering that little Taber girl."

There was fondness in his voice; that stopped me.

"Wasn't Janet blackmailing you, Mr. Norman?"

"Blackmailing ... ?" A dry rasp sounded in his throat: his laugh. "No, no, Stefan knew that wasn't so, or he at least *should* have. Still, I suppose he meant well."

"I'm ... sure he did."

"But it was so silly of him, so silly to think she was taking advantage of me. Why, I doubt she even knew of me, I kept in the background so. Stefan should have known better."

"He should have?"

"Why, of course. He was the one I had contact the girl's mother, he better than anyone knew how badly I wanted to find the girl, and then how pleased I was when, after several years had dragged by, she turned up again."

"Why did you want to see her, Mr. Norman? Why would you search for Janet Taber?"

He waved a quavery hand in the air, like the reluctant blessing of a disillusioned old priest. "That doesn't matter, not now...."

"Oh?"

"She's dead. And her son's dead."

"Her son?" And I remembered Janet's little boy and his heart trouble and the anonymous benefactor. "You were helping Janet help her son? Did you arrange for his treatment at a clinic in the east?"

He nodded. "But none of that matters. She's dead. Her son is dead."

"Her son," I said.

"Her son," he said. "Hers and Richard's."

I looked out the window; it caught the reflection of the smiling portrait behind us.

"My grandson," he said. Softly. Softly.

TWENTY-FIVE

Harold was waiting for me at the bottom of the stairwell. He seemed too big to fit within the walls: he was a ship in a bottle and I wondered how it was done. He said, "How's Mr. Norman?"

"He's all right. I helped him back to bed."

"You didn't make things worse for him?"

"I'm not sure that'd be possible," I said. "Let's go somewhere and talk."

He said, "I sent Rita across the street for some groceries and when she gets back she's going to fix us breakfast. That should give us time to discuss things."

"You were expecting this?"

"Of course," he said. "Weren't you?"

He led me into the empty living room, where the sun was slanting in through the many odd-shaped, undraped windows like swords stuck in a magician's box. Our footsteps clomped, but didn't echo. Harold gestured toward an arched doorway and I went on through it and he followed. We walked across the dead lawn and stopped a few yards from the drop-off. The river was choppy today; a gray barge was riding down to the lock and dam and wasn't having an easy time of it. There was a crisp breeze and I wished I had worn a jacket.

"Rita says you write mystery stories," Harold said, looking out toward the river.

"That's right."

He looked at me; the one eye bored into me. "You think life's a mystery story?"

"What do you mean?"

"That tidy. That neat. That easy to deal with."

I shrugged. "No. But life is *like* a mystery story, sometimes. Full of secrets somebody's trying to keep, and can't. Or anyway shouldn't."

He grunted; his breath smoked in the cold air, like the exhaust of a car. "My life isn't a damn mystery story. Anyway it's not *your* damn mystery story."

"Maybe not," I said. "But I'm in it."

He thought about that. Nodded. "I guess you are."

"Why don't you tell me, Harold?"

"You're the mystery writer. You tell me."

"All right. I'll tell you a story. It might not be much more than a story, but I'll give it a whirl."

He grunted again.

"Once upon a time," I began, "there was a senator named Richard Norman. And this senator had an affair with a secretary of his called Janet Ferris. It might've started at his senate office in Des Moines; but it wound up in Port City, probably in a motel room, during the summer the senator was launching his campaign for national office."

Harold just stood and listened, impassive as a rock.

"The senator had a wife, too, but she was pregnant at the time—very pregnant. She delivered a baby girl to the senator late that summer. Maybe it was during those last few months of the wife's pregnancy that the senator finally gave in to the secretary, and what might have started as a simple flirtation turned into something more complex, more complex than just another affair, too. Because the secretary also got pregnant.

"Now I don't know whether the senator told his wife about the pregnant secretary. I kind of doubt it. But I'm pretty sure he would've told his political advisor, monetary backer and guiding light behind everything he did: his father, Simon Norman. The man behind the man. And I'm pretty sure I know how Sy Norman would've handled the secretary: he would pay her off to go away quietly and just disappear.

"And she did. She went off to Old Town in Chicago and was a hippie with her hippie husband for a while, quite good and soured on an Establishment she'd briefly believed in. How am I doing, Harold?"

When Harold answered, I was almost surprised: it was like the rock suddenly talked. "It's your story," he shrugged.

"Is it? Anyway, a few years pass and in the midst of launching a second attempt to go to Washington, the senator dies in a car crash. So does his wife. And so does his only child—the only legitimate child, that is. Old Sy Norman has a stroke shortly after. And then someone remembered the pregnant secretary, and reminded the old man about her; perhaps she hadn't had an abortion—perhaps she'd *had* the child.

"And so the Norman forces tracked down Janet Taber; or anyway, tracked down Janet's mother. And it turned out Janet had indeed had the child, a son. A grandson for Sy Norman. Something that would outlive him. Something that came from him that would last. For some reason, Janet's mother was used as a go-between. Was it because Janet was bitter toward the Normans? Could it be that the other time Janet had *turned down* the money they offered her, and had just disappeared into

Old Town and became a hippie, snubbing their capitalistic offer?"

Harold turned his gaze on me and nodded.

"Okay, then. It starts to make sense. The mother acted as go-between; Janet suspected who was behind it, but since her child needed medical care, she went along—maybe lied to herself that it *wasn't* the Normans paying the bills. Hoping it was some other good-hearted John Beresford Tipton type. Maybe it was easier for her to live with it that way. Whatever the case, whatever the reasons, she went along with it, and her son went to that clinic in the east.

"And now I have to guess. I can only guess. But I'm almost sure I'm right. A day or two before you pulled your scare tactic on Janet at the bus station, Harold—and why exactly you did that, I admit I'm still not sure of—a day or two before things started getting ugly, the boy died."

Harold again turned his gaze on me. Again he nodded slowly. Sadly.

"I thought so! The little boy in the big fancy clinic died. But Janet Taber never knew that. She was never told. That's something, anyway; that's a burden she didn't have to carry to her grave with her. But that's about the only break she got. Because Stefan—and his killing machine, Davis—had decided to get rid of both

Janet and her mother, before they found
out the boy was dead."

"And why would they do that, Mallory?"

I poked his barrel chest with a finger.
"Because Janet and her son were both in
the old man's will! Am I right? Because
Stefan wanted it *all*, and because news of
the grandson's death might kill the old
man, and then Stefan would lose a good
chunk of his inheritance. So Stefan had to
act fast—a fire, a car crash—and then he
stood to inherit it all again. Pretty sloppy
work, if you ask me, but then it helps to
have the local cops in your pocket when
you're doing work as clumsy as it is
ruthless."

Harold laughed humorlessly. "Stefan was
a clumsy criminal. He was a manipulator,
a schemer—but when it came to murder,
he was out of his depth."

"So much so that he ended up committing suicide."

"Right. But the blame for that is *yours*,
Mallory."

"Mine?"

"Stefan's clumsy staging of 'accidents'
would've held up, but for you. Like you
said, the police and the sheriff are in the
Norman family's pocket; the investigations
of these events would've been cursory, at
best. How was Stefan to know a . . . a
mystery writer like yourself would be on
hand to poke in here, and unravel there?"

The elation I'd been feeling, from putting the pieces together, suddenly faded; the wind was cold on my face but the sun had come out from under some clouds and made me squint.

I said, "So when the holes in Stefan's not-so-grand design began to show and the local law *had* to start looking into things, and when his roommate Davis ended up dying for him—when it all began coming apart and falling in on him—he had an attack of despair and wrote a self-serving suicide note, apparently designed to spare his uncle's feelings, a bit, and then put a bullet in his brain."

Harold nodded. The barge horn blew, a foghorn sound.

"Bullshit," I said. "You killed Stefan, Harold. Why don't you just tell me about it? It is *your* story, after all. . . ."

TWENTY-SIX

"You have to understand about Stefan Norman," Harold said. "Stefan Norman was a snake."

His voice was a dry whisper; so was the wind.

"Stefan Norman," Harold went on, "was the one who told Richard Norman's wife about her husband and his secretary and a baby that might or might not have been aborted. And Mrs. Norman, she didn't take it so well. She developed . . . nervous trouble. Then she developed drinking trouble. Psychoanalysis didn't seem to help either problem. She proved a constant sourse of embarrassment for the Normans during the senator's second national campaign. Rumors about her, which she in one way or another managed to generate, were so ugly that most people refused to believe them. Dismissed them as vicious smears. Like the one about her trying to drown their daughter while vacationing at Lake Okoboji."

"Jesus," I said.

Harold sighed heavily. "How the senator felt about his wife at this point I can't really say. At one time he and I were rather close. He often revealed personal things to me, but . . . but when the business with his wife's drinking and her cruelty to their daughter began, the senator clammed up."

"What in hell possessed Richard Norman to get drunk and drive his car off Colorado Hill? It wasn't suicide, was it?"

Harold said nothing.

"I get it," I said. "Richard wasn't driving that night. Richard wasn't the drunk behind the wheel, was he? It was the wife. The wife."

Harold nodded, said, "But the senator *did* allow his wife to drive back from Davenport when she was so drunk she could barely walk, let alone steer a car."

"So what are you saying? That Richard Norman handing his wife the wheel was like handing her a revolver and saying shoot?"

Harold was looking past the drop-off before us, at the river. "Stefan felt that that interpretation of the events was likely, so likely that he advised Mr. Norman to go to the trouble of instructing the local authorities to have all the reports state that the senator was driving. Still, there were those who guessed past the cover-up that followed—those who guessed that Mrs. Norman had been driving, and who *just knew* she'd been steering accurately when she drove that car over Colorado Hill."

Then he turned his one eye and his black eyepatch on me and said, "But they're just guessing. And so are we."

"What do *you* think, Harold? You and the senator were close, you said."

"I don't believe the death of his family was a conscious wish on the senator's part. Maybe he hated his wife by this time; I don't know. And he may have hated himself; that I don't know, either. But he loved his little daughter. *That* much I do know."

"Somebody else loved the daughter, too," I said, gesturing with a thumb back at the house.

"Yes," Harold nodded. "Mr. Norman loved the little girl. He used to say the little girl would grow up to be 'the spittin' image' of his late wife. I feel it was the loss of the grandchild that triggered Mr. Norman's stroke, more than losing his son the senator."

"Who was it that remembered the other grandchild, Janet Taber's illegitimate child? Stefan?"

Harold laughed; it was a deep, throaty laugh, and came as a shock, as he'd been speaking in hushed tones till now.

"Hardly," he said. "Why would Stefan remind his uncle of another possible heir? *I* reminded Mr. Norman about the pregnant secretary. And it was the chance that a grandchild of his might be alive somewhere that made Simon Harrison Norman want to *live* again. And when the recovery had taken an upward turn, he *spoke* again, the first time since the stroke; he spoke to Stefan." He laughed again. "Ordered his sole heir to search for the child."

"Stefan wasn't crazy about that, I assume."

"No," Harold smiled. "Stefan could hardly be expected to take pleasure in a search that would result in a decrease in his share of the Norman inheritance. But he went through the motions. He hired the necessary investigators and went himself to Des Moines to visit the girl's mother, who hadn't seen her daughter for several years, at that point."

"And for a while that was as far as the search got."

"Right. Mr. Norman got on Stefan's case about it, from time to time, and once when Stefan said to his uncle that the search was useless because 'the damn thing was probably aborted anyway,' the old man flew into a rage. I suspected that Stefan was doing this to provoke another stroke—a fatal one—so I had words with him."

"What kind of words?"

"Convincing words," Harold said.

Harold was pressing his hands together in front of him, squeezing, like a vise of flesh. I was reminded for a moment that despite Harold's gentle, genteel manner, this was *still* Punjab, still the one-eyed massive bear that I'd butted heads with at the bus station not so long ago.

"Finally," Harold said, almost ignoring me, "Mrs. Ferris contacted Mr. Norman. Her daughter had phoned her, finally, with a tearful story of a critically ill child. And Mr. Norman—through Stefan—arranged for Mrs. Ferris to bring Janet to Port City to live, where they could be looked after. Mr. Norman thought it best to remain anonymous, being wary of the young woman's once before having refused Norman money."

"And old Sy Norman changed his will," I said. "Which Stefan didn't like one little bit."

Nodding, Harold said, "First the young boy was written in, though a third of the estate would still go to Stefan, and Stefan would be executor, in charge of the boy's funds *and* the Norman Fund, until the child reached twenty-one. But by then Mr. Norman had started thinking of Janet Taber as his late son's 'other wife,' as the woman who shared his son's love—shared it more than that 'miserable bitch' who drove him off a cliff, anyway."

"And so Janet was written into the will, too," I said. "And made her son's executor?"

"Yes," Harold said. "She was second in importance only to the grandchild himself. And stood to gain control of the Norman Fund, as well."

I thought that over. "Stefan had already been forced to turn the will's leading role over to the child," I said, a little breathlessly, putting it together. "Now he was reduced from co-star to supporting player. After years of controlling the Norman money through the Fund, answering only to a bedridden, near-senile old man, he now had to deal with young, intelligent Janet Taber, not to mention her shrewd momma. Or the lawyers and accountants they'd bring with 'em during the takeover. And maybe Stefan's books for the Fund weren't any better balanced than Richard Norman's wife when she drove off Colorado Hill, hmmm?"

Harold was shaking his head, and it wasn't in a "no" gesture; he said, "You *are* a mystery writer, aren't you?"

"Am I wrong?"

"Did I say you were? I told you Stefan was a snake. I always knew that. But I didn't know to what extent, until I found he was putting together evidence designed to prove to Mr. Norman that the child was the offspring of Janet's hippie, common-law husband."

"Phil Taber," I nodded. "So he and Stefan *were* connected."

"Very much so. Taber had been going with Janet at Drake before the summer she and the senator . . . well. It was not a farfetched notion that Taber could've been the child's father. In fact, Stefan came to me with his evidence first. Stefan knew Mr. Norman valued my opinion, trusted me as he trusted no other. So he used me as a guinea pig, though I didn't know that at the time. I looked at the signed state-ment Phil Taber had made, and motel registration slips and so on, and I was convinced that the child was quite likely Taber's. I begged Stefan not to show Mr. Norman the evidence! I felt it would only serve to demoralize Mr. Norman, perhaps even cause another stroke. I suggested to Stefan that he wait till after Mr. Simon had passed away; the evidence could then be used to contest the will, rather than now, when it would only serve to hurt the old man. And Stefan agreed to wait."

"Why?"

Harold's laugh was short, sarcastic. "I thought—just for a moment, mind you— that he had found some compassion for his uncle, somewhere. It's only recently become obvious that Stefan agreed to wait only because he was *creating* evidence, not just amassing it, and he didn't have enough of it put together for it to hold up under a court's scrutiny. I am convinced now that the child was indeed the senator's, or Stefan would've moved on it sooner."

"When was all this?"

"Not long ago. A few months. And then this past Monday afternoon, a call came from the clinic out east: the boy was dead. Stefan took the call. Janet and her mother were not told. Mr. Norman was. He took it hard, as you would expect. You've seen him. He's slipping away."

"How did Stefan take it?"

Harold's face turned cold. "Stefan went to Mrs. Ferris and offered her a considerable sum for her defection—the mother wasn't in the Norman will, after all, and Stefan felt Mrs. Ferris was, therefore, vulnerable. It's a common mistake of a snake like Stefan, to assume that the rest of humanity is as greedy and vile as he is."

Harold was getting worked up; he was telling me things he had no firsthand way to know—things that only Stefan could have told him. . . .

Harold went on, almost as if I wasn't there: "Stefan hoped Mrs. Ferris would help him convince her daughter to make a signed 'admission' that the son was Taber's, not the senator's. Stefan had to move fast; he couldn't keep the child's death a secret forever, you know. So he offered Mrs. Ferris a lot of money—I don't know how much, that he didn't say. 'Generous financial settlement,' he told me, but who knows what that amounted to, in Stefan's mind? But one of the things he did promise—and this tells you all you need to know about Stefan Norman—he promised as a fringe benefit continued clinical treatment for the child." Harold's eye was wet. "Continued clinical treatment. For a little boy already dead." He clenched both fists. Suddenly I wasn't nuts about standing on the edge of a drop-off with this guy.

"Mrs. Ferris and her daughter," he said, "were to leave Port City at once. For good. Only it didn't work out that way. Mrs. Ferris rejected Stefan's overtures, and Stefan must've lapsed into hysteria, or violence, or something, because the upshot was the larger Mrs. Ferris was flailing the smaller Stefan, at which point Stefan's friend Davis, waiting outside, heard the commotion, stepped in and beat her to death. The two men then set the fire, using old rags and paint cans on the back porch for fuel."

"And then that left only Janet to take care of," I said.

Harold covered his face with one large hand, briefly, then looked at me; it's funny how an eyepatch can seem to stare at you just like an eye can.

"I feel . . . sick when I think of my role in this. I had so bought Stefan's bill of goods, I so believed that Janet Taber was a 'blackmailing bitch,' so believed that her child was Taber's, not the senator's, that I went looking for her, the Tuesday morning after the fire. You see, I knew there'd been a fire, and her mother hospitalized, but I didn't know the mother had been *beaten*. I knew only that there had been a fire, and, naively, I assumed it was accidental. A dangerous assumption, with Stefan around. And, to my discredit, I thought Janet's distressed condition would only make her more impressionable, more easily swayed. And so, I staged that ridiculous show at the bus terminal. To scare her off, to scare her off once and for all."

"So that wasn't Stefan's idea."

"That was my own doing; he knew nothing of it. In fact, we were working at cross purposes, but didn't know it. Stefan had told me that Janet Taber's only reaction to the death of her child was to say that if she was in any way denied what she felt she had coming to her, she would malign the late senator publicly and drag the Normans thoroughly through the mud. I felt Mr. Norman had been put through

enough already and hoped to put a scare
into her, to convince her to leave Port City
and any claims on Mr. Norman behind."

"But it didn't work."

"Thanks to you, Mallory. But do you
realize if I'd been successful in scaring her
off, she might still be alive? If she'd been
fearful enough to grab a bus to points
unknown instead of staying around? Do
you realize that if you hadn't gotten involved, she might not have died?"

He was right. By trying to help, I'd hurt.
In a weird, roundabout way, I'd done as
much to contribute to the death of Janet
Taber as anybody!

Then Harold said, as if on some sort of
automatic pilot, not wanting to hear the
words he was speaking, "Janet Taber's
'accident' was hastily planned, but came
off smoothly enough. Davis met the young
woman as she got off her bus in Iowa City,
telling her he was a plainclothes officer
there to escort her to the hospital to see
her mother. Once he had her in the car, he
chloroformed her and broke her neck and
. . . maybe she did see her mother, after
all; but not in this world."

His voice was so hushed I could barely
hear him now.

"The . . . accident . . . at Colorado Hill
was staged in the hope Mr. Norman would
assume his son's 'other wife' had taken her

life at the site of the death of her 'husband'
—her 'suicide' there might seem the ulti-
mate expression of sorrow over the loss of
the son she bore her 'lost love.'"

I felt weak, sick, dizzy; but somehow my
brain kept up with all of it, and I heard
myself saying, "So that's the Colorado Hill
connection, but that seems like such half-
assed logic to me. And risky. Why connect
Janet's death to the senator's? Just for the
old man's benefit? It's crazy."

Harold shrugged. "Stefan knew how his
uncle's mind worked. Mr. Norman backed
Stefan and hushed the two deaths up, all
the way. If nothing else, Mr. Norman knew
what kind of unpleasant memories stood
to be unearthed by a full-scale investigation of Janet Taber's death. So such an
inquiry was to be avoided. Stefan knew
what he was doing."

"The son of a bitch."

"I told you what kind of man he was,"
Harold said. "A snake."

Harold stared out over the drop-off; I
stared at Harold.

"When did he tell you all this, Harold?"

He didn't answer.

I went on: "'Oh, but that's obvious—it
was right before you killed him."

Without turning to look at me, he said,
flatly, "I didn't say I killed him, Mallory."

"You didn't have to."

Harold turned his head, not his body,

and smiled at me; it was a smile that had no humor in it, just secrets. Harold still had secrets.

"Maybe I didn't kill him, Mallory," he said.

And then Rita's voice, sounding far away, called out to us.

TWENTY-SEVEN

"Hey!" she yelled.

She was coming across the brown grass, coming to meet us, and she was smiling and looking very pretty, very fresh, incongruously so against the image of the bleak gray house looming up back of her.

We stood there awkwardly, Harold and I, like actors who couldn't remember their lines, and waited for her to join us. She latched onto Harold by the hand and me the same and tugged at us, saying, "You two gonna come in and eat the breakfast you had me cook, or do you like your eggs cold?"

So we turned and walked with her back across the lawn and into the house, turning left as we entered the living room and going through a doorless archway into the wing adjacent to Harold's room. She deposited us in a breakfast nook, a cubbyhole stuck between the pantry and kitchen and filled by a wooden booth painted with once-vivid colors in a vaguely Scandinavian pattern. The colors in the kitchen area were the brightest in the house, with pale blue walls instead of cream, and with the dimmed reds and blues and yellows of the painted booth in the midst of it.

I sat and stared across at Harold and the air was thick with things unsaid. There wasn't any purpose in saying them, after all. I looked at Harold and Harold's single solemn eye and his black patch looked back at me and we knew.

I knew, Harold knew, that Stefan Norman had handled the Mallory problem in the same manner he'd handled the Renata Ferris problem, and that of Janet Taber as well: he'd dispatched Davis, that violent extension of himself, to do his work. Stefan had had no compunction about treating human lives like so many pieces on a chessboard: he was the chessmaster and I was just another pawn for him to send his queen out to get. And even if his queen fell, suicide was not Stefan's style, not in his makeup.

Harold knew all this. No need for me to tell him.

Rita came in and put a plate down in front of each of us, scooched in next to me on my side of the booth. I looked down at the omelet and the hash browns and the toast and knew I would have trouble getting it down, knew also that I had to. "Oh damn," Rita said, and got up and went into the kitchen and came back with coffee and filled our cups.

I poked around at the plate of food, and Harold did likewise, but between bites we exchanged looks, continued our silent conversation.

Harold knew, as I do, as you do, that suicide says despair, that suicide means finality, and a man in despair doesn't change the facts around "a little" in what amounts to a deathbed confession of murder, just to make himself look a shade less corrupt. He might make excuses, he might even lie to himself, he might rationalize; but shape a slightly different, slightly juggled, slightly edited, slightly more excusable explanation, before putting a gun to his head? Please.

Neither would Stefan be likely to care about sparing old Sy Norman's feelings.

But Harold would.

Harold had made no secret of his loyalty to Mr. Norman, and had expressed it in no less tangible and eccentric a manner than my first meeting with him when he tried, for the sake of his elderly employer, to scare Janet Taber out of town.

But that was when he was under the mistaken impression that Janet was a "blackmailing bitch," that was when he was still caught up in the various machinations of Stefan's plotting. Somewhere recently along the line, Harold had seen through Stefan, Harold had stopped being conned by him and that intense loyalty for Mr. Norman, that fierce protective instinct for the old man who had done so much for him, was channeled into a concentrated effort by Harold to put a stop to Stefan Norman's scheming.

In my mind, I could see it: Harold stands beside Stefan, holding Stefan's own gun over him, dictates the "suicide note"; Stefan sits at the desk, takes it all down, sweats as the black, one-eyed apparition hovers over him; the note is finished and Harold shoots Stefan; Stefan falls limp across the desk, like the inanimate object he has become.

"More coffee?" Rita said.

"Please," I said.

"Harold?"

Harold nodded.

I managed to finish the eggs and potatoes and toast and when I glanced over at Harold, he had done the same. Rita came back, poured refills on coffee, and joined us. Harold and I sipped at the cups, looking away from each other when approaching a stare.

Rita was finally beginning to suspect something was wrong, because the silence hung heavy, like a tapestry pulling at its nails, and as the anxiety began to show on her face, I ventured with, "Fine breakfast, Rita, really fine," and Harold said, "Yes, yes it is, it's fine."

She smiled. "I guess I can understand you boys being so quiet. This whole affair has been a real drain on us all—physically and emotionally both. You wouldn't believe how *relieved* I am it's over."

"I am pretty tired," I said.

"You should be," she said. "You been up practically all night." She reached across the table and patted her brother's pawlike hand and said, "How 'bout you, bro? You feeling it yet?"

"I could use some sleep," he said.

"Did you get back to bed this morning after I called you?" she asked him. "You haven't been up all this time, have you?"

"I went back to bed," he said.

I said, "Rita, you called Harold? When?"

"After you called me, when that guy . . . what was his name? The guy who broke in."

"Davis."

"Yeah, him. After you called me, when Davis was killed. I wanted to prove to old hardhead Harold here that you and I *weren't* paranoid, that somebody *was* going 'round doing those things we told him about."

She smiled embarrassedly at her brother. "And frankly, Harold, I was relieved that you weren't involved, 'cause Mal was entertaining thoughts you might be one of the bad guys. And you *did* seem mad at me for bringing him here to see you last night."

I said, "Say Rita, all of a sudden I'm really hungry. You got any more of those hash browns?"

"Hungry? You serious, Mal? Hell, you just poked at your food."

"No, really, I'm just starting to wake up. I always get hungry when I start waking up. And those hash browns hit the spot."

"I could whip up some more, I guess."

"Would you, please?"

She shrugged. "Okay. Harold, how about you?"

Harold said, "Fine."

She rose from the booth and disappeared around the corner into the kitchen.

I spoke softly, a near-whisper. I said, "You want to tell me . . . I think I know, but do you want to tell me?"

Just as softly, Harold said, "If you know it, tell it, mystery writer."

"All right. All right. We'll start in where Rita called you and told you how a guy named Davis busted into my trailer and ended up dead. That was the breaking point, am I right? When Stefan went so far as putting your own sister in danger?"

Harold didn't say anything. He was going to make me do it all.

I said, "You probably already had your mind made up to have it out with Stefan, just from the things I'd told you about him. Things like his denying he knew Janet Taber, his denying even that he knew *you*. And then there was that business of Phil Taber being in town, five thousand bucks richer than before he came, last payment for services rendered to one Stefan Norman. This time Taber was getting paid off for seeing that Janet and her mom got shoved under the ground as soon as possible. But he'd been paid by Stefan Norman before."

Harold remained silent. He wasn't going to give me any help at all.

I said, "So what happened, after Rita called you? Did you try Stefan's Davenport number and get no answer? And then did you try his office number here in town, and he was there, but waiting for a call? Did he answer the phone saying something like ... 'Davis, how did it go?' "

Harold stirred.

"And what then? Hell, why bother? We both know what happened after that."

"It wasn't what you think. It wasn't that way."

"Sure it was. You got Stefan's gun out of his room here in the house. Then you went down to the Maxwell Buiding, went up to the Fund office and held Stefan at gun-point and told him what to put in the note. *Somebody* had to have told Stefan about Davis's death—I figured maybe Bren-nan or one of the local cops had. But it was *you*, Harold. You. You shot him."

"You know what the trouble with you is, Mallory?"

"No. Tell me."

"You don't think. You put things to-gether, but you don't think. Did you read the note?"

"You know I did."

"Did it sound like a suicide note?"

"It sounded like a phony suicide note."

"Did it even sound like that? Did it even sound like a convincing fake?"

I didn't know what he was getting at and said so.

He said, "It was a confession. I made him write a confession, can't you see that? You can see the rest, why can't you see that it wasn't meant to be a suicide note, not when I had him write it."

"A confession."

"A confession. What I wanted from Ste-fan was a written statement of guilt, some-thing I'd have to hang over him. The sword of Damocles, ever hear of that? I had to keep him in line. Make sure he didn't go pulling any more stunts. Make sure he didn't make miserable what little there is left of Mr. Norman's life."

"But it wasn't an accurate confession. . . ."

"Of course not. I wanted a confession that would give Mr. Norman the least possible pain, but still would be damning to Stefan. Do you think I wanted Stefan's suicide? Do you think Stefan's suicide is the kind of thing I'd want to put Mr. Norman through?"

"Stefan *is* dead, Harold."

"Yes, he is."

"So something went wrong."

"You might say that."

"What? How?"

"Once he got it written, I told Stefan what I planned to do with the note. I told him it was going to be sealed in an envelope and given to a lawyer, with instructions to open it either at my death or my request, whatever came first. After that, when Stefan knew that, that was when he got stupid."

"And tried to take the gun away from you."

"And tried to take the gun away from me."

"And, in the struggle . . . ?"

"In the struggle."

We sat and looked at each other.

Then I said, "And you left the confession there, to make do as a suicide note?"

"Yes."

"Well," I said. "So now I know."

Harold smiled on one side of his face. "So now you know it all. How's it make you feel, mystery writer? All satisfied inside?"

Rita came in and set down a dish of hash browns and said, "Here's your seconds."

Before we finished eating, Rita went back out to the kitchen for some more coffee, and Harold said, "Mallory?"

"Yeah?"

"What I told you . . . you believe me?"

"Yeah."

"There's no way Brennan's going to figure it out, and even if he does, he's not going to prove anything. Or want to. Not with Davis dead. Funny."

"What?"

"Stefan wept when I told him Davis was dead. I didn't know Stefan had it in him. But it must've made him a little bit suicidal at that."

I sipped my coffee.

"Mallory?"

"Yeah?"

"What're you going to do now?"

"Finish my eggs."

"And then?"

"Drive your sister home."

"That all?"

"No. I'll probably try and get some sleep. I'm feeling tired."

Harold nodded. "I know what you mean."

Rita came back in and filled our cups and we finished our food and coffee and soon she and I were getting into the Rambler and Harold was standing, filling the back doorway, like something permanent in the house, watching us go.

PART FIVE

DECEMBER 24, 1974

CHRISTMAS EVE

TWENTY-EIGHT

I looked down at the picture on the cardboard container. Turkey with dressing and potatoes and peas, buttered, with a smidgen of cranberry sauce, garnished with parsley, served on a china plate. I took the cold aluminum tray out and closed it up in the oven, set the heat on four hundred and the timer for thirty minutes. On my way to the couch I got myself a Pabst.

If you ever spent Christmas Eve alone, you know the kind of depressed I was. And putting John on the plane this afternoon hadn't helped any.

I'd spent the better part of the rest of John's leave trying to convince him *not* to get back in the Indochina soup like a good li'l fly. But he said it was too late for him to get out of it, said I might as well get off his back, the papers were all signed, but I had a feeling he wasn't leveling: I had a feeling if he'd come home to something that seemed like home to him, he might've stayed. But Suzie Blanchard was seeing her ex-husband again, and his stepfather had been a big disappointment, and he'd killed a man.

So last night we got drunk on red wine, and I didn't say a word about any of it, and he likewise gave me a period of grace, not saying anything about the Janet Taber/Sy Norman matter, which was still a sore spot for me.

Because John had been right the first time: solving Janet Taber's "mystery" hadn't made either her *or* me rest any easier. I thought finding "the truth" would help her in some vague metaphysical way, but it didn't, because the kind of truth I found was one-dimensional; there was another kind of truth that couldn't be gotten at, because the clues to it were the skeletons of events from lives that weren't being lived anymore, because it was a truth locked way in the minds, the psyches, of dead people.

The puzzle pieces had been made to fit, and the surface level was now a picture you could look at, but what was underneath was something neither I nor anyone else could ever know. There were people involved I hadn't ever met, people who were dead before I got there. I didn't know the name of Richard Norman's wife, for instance. Or the name of his little girl. I'd read their obituaries, but their names hadn't seemed important enough to bother remembering.

For that matter, I didn't know Richard Norman beyond his name, really. Or Janet Taber's mother. Or Janet Taber, if you got right down to it.

I'd met her, but I didn't know her.

I'd met Stefan, but I didn't know him. Oh yes, he was the bad guy, he was who the killer turned out to be, and his killing machine was a man named Davis. But I couldn't know what it was in Stefan Norman that let him have people killed, just as I couldn't know what it was in Stefan Norman that made him weep for Davis. Or what it was in Davis that made him worth weeping for.

But these were thoughts. They didn't get said. I was too drunk to articulate them and John was too drunk to understand them.

Later on, drunker still, he said, "You oughta call Rita."

And I said I'd get around to it.

I had decided not to see Rita for a while, at least till the circumstances that brought us together had faded in my memory a little. Before, when John had first asked me about it, I'd said I broke it off early because of the hassles I figured a racially mixed couple would run into in this part of the country. But that wasn't it. It was her brother maybe, things about him I knew that she didn't, and a time of my life I was trying to put out of mind, even though she was a very pleasant part of that time. I'd see her later. Call her sometime.

I asked John why he wasn't spending his last evening with Suzie Blanchard and he made a face and that's when he told me her ex-husband had dropped around today and she was busy.

About then we started the second bottle and lots of things got forgotten.

By this afternoon, when I drove him up to the airport, he wasn't John anymore. He was wearing his dress uniform and his hair was fresh-cropped and he sat rigid in his seat like a cardboard cutout. He was slowly being sucked back into that other person he was in that other world.

Brennan had offered to drive John to the airport, but John turned him down. That hurt Brennan, and I almost found myself wanting to make peace between them, but now wasn't the time. John had idolized the guy for years, looked up to him as a "man's man"; going into the Army right out of high school had been, partially at least, an effort by John to please his often remote stepfather. And now John had learned the facts of Brennan's life, complete with politics and graft and imperfections, and was disillusioned. He wouldn't be calling Brennan "sir" anymore. Not for a long while, anyway.

So I had driven him and now we sat and waited for his plane. The airport was swarming with people trying to get places for Christmas and we had little privacy. A young woman and her baby crowded me in the next seat, and a sailor was running his cap around in his hands in the seat next to John. Outside it was dark, though it was only around four; the darkness was clouds, mostly, and John pointed out at them and said, "Hope that doesn't mean my flight's going to be delayed."

"Maybe so," I said. "Maybe it's going to snow. I kind of hope it does. Christmas isn't Christmas without it."

And that was pretty much the way the rest of our conversation went. Degenerated into impersonal chitchat. Once, when I asked John about where he'd take his R and R, he brightened momentarily and said he thought he'd go back to Bangkok and look up the girl he'd been with last time.

But soon he was sitting rigidly again,

and then the plane was there and I had to watch him walk through a door where his ticket was checked and he disappeared. I went quickly out another door and got on the other side of the fence behind which John was walking toward the big silver jet, marching into the artificial wind of its exhaust. For a while I didn't think he'd turn to look back, and when he finally did, about halfway between me and the jet, he didn't wave or anything: he just let the John part of him take hold of his face for a second and he gave me that pained look friends give each other when they maybe aren't going to see each other again.

I stood there and watched the jet go through its motions, the taxiing around, the takeoff, its exhausts screaming hot, hoarse, and then I stood there and watched some other jets do the same things. After a while it started to snow.

The timer went off and I went to the oven and got the TV dinner out. I lifted the foil off and the steam came up and hit me in the face and I walked the hot tray over to the sink and dumped its contents into the mouth of the garbage disposal.

I went over to a window and looked out. The snow had stopped already, but it was cold enough to keep the ground white.

I wondered if any restaurants were open Christmas Eve.

I got another Pabst and flopped on the couch.

The phone rang.

I grabbed the receiver off the hook, hostile at having my depression interrupted, and told myself not to be surly, after all, it's Christmas Eve, and said, "Yeah?"

"Hi, stranger."

Rita.

"Hi."

"You wouldn't know where a lady could find some holiday company, would you? I don't think I can face a TV dinner all by myself."

I smiled.

"Mal?"

"I'm smiling," I said.

"You got people there? Am I butting into something?"

"Not at all."

"I was hoping you weren't busy, 'cause I been . . . dreaming of a white Christmas, if you know what I mean."

I laughed. "Where are you?"

"Give you a hint: the walls are purple."

"I'm on my way."

I hung up, grabbed my coat, my keys.

I let the Rambler take off in the direction its nose was pointing, and thirty seconds later I was sitting at the stop sign, waiting to get onto Grand Street, waiting for traffic to subside and let me in so I could head for one of the two possible routes to the Quad Cities. Left lane traffic lulled and I had time to make it, but that would put me in the direction of the River Road, the scenic route along the Mississippi, over Colorado Hill. I waited and pulled out the other way.

EPILOGUE

1983

TWENTY-NINE

John was killed in 1975, while flying with Air America, during the evacuation of Vietnam.

Sy Norman died the same year; he left his house to the city, assuming the place would be turned into a museum. He should have so stipulated in his will, because when the new high bridge went in, in 1979, the city had the house torn down and a small open park put in its place, overlooking the river. A small plaque mentions Doc Norman and his cancer clinic and radio station; a larger plaque mentions Mark Twain and his penchant for Port City sunsets—the park is named Mark Twain Overlook.

Harold was remembered well in Norman's will; and Rita—who is teaching full-time now, at a community college in

Elgin, Illinois—says he's opened a big-and-tall men's shop in suburban Chicago.

Brennan is still sheriff; Jack Masters, Lori and the rest are still in the area, like me.

And as for me, I finally got around to writing that mystery novel, didn't I?